A DOGGONE DEATH

---

a Samantha Davies mystery

S.A. Kazlo

In life I feel a person is lucky to have one true friend. I am blessed to have two. Thank you, Sharon Jensen and Sue Carrigan for always being there for me. Let's pull some loops.

Acknowledgements

Once again it has taken quite a few people to make this book happen. I'm especially grateful to the following people for their time and help.

June Kosier for being my Beta reader extraordinaire.

My undying gratitude to my two critique groups for their invaluable help:
The GFWG—Zack Richards, Billy Neary, AJ Davidson. Bill Thomas, Kay Hafner, Robin Inwald, Sandy Buxton, Jackie Goodwin, Montana Tracy, Alan Schroeder Jr.
The Storyboarders—Roxyanne Young, Lisa Rondinelli Alberts, and Candie Moonshower
I'm forever grateful to my publisher—Gemma Halliday for bringing Sam and Porkchop to life and for Jennifer Rarden and her terrific editing.

Most of all I want to thank my biggest fan and cheerleader—my wonderful husband, Michael. Thank you for all of your support and love.

CHAPTER ONE

———

"My poor Precious!" Candie moaned. "This snow is ruining her new wax job! I never fussed about her finish in Tennessee."

I laughed. "Candie, you and Precious moved north fifteen years ago after breaking up with, what fiancé number was he? You live in upstate New York. It always snows in March. Salt and grime on your car are a given."

She waved bejeweled fingers at me. *Bling* was her middle name. "Hubert was number eleven, but who's counting. Gad night a livin'! Where am I going to park Precious?"

Precious was my dear Southern cousin's baby—a light blue '73 Mustang convertible. "I'll let you and our equipment off at the door and check behind the firehouse for parking." Good thought on Candie's part, as I wasn't about to lug a rug hooking frame and all things necessary for our addictive hobby farther than necessary. Hookers didn't travel light. A Sherpa carried less equipment up Mount Everest.

I stretched my neck to peer through Precious's snow-splotched windshield. "I'm thrilled for Lucy. Her hook-in looks like a success if the packed parking lot is any indication." Our good friend, Lucy Foster, was holding her first annual The Ewe and Me hook-in in the banquet hall attached to the Wings Fall Fire Company. The room often hosted wedding receptions and large parties. The rentals provided a much-needed source of income for the fire company. The news of Lucy's hook-in had buzzed through the local rug hooking groups, and by the license plates on the parked cars, attendees had traveled from all the surrounding states. Promise a hooker good food and vendors who satisfied their wool habit, and they'd follow you anywhere.

Candie pulled up to the front door of the banquet hall. I reached into the back seat of the Mustang and pulled out two large tote bags containing our rug hooking gear—a frame, hook, scissors, pattern, and wool strips. I stepped out of Precious and watched as the car's taillights disappeared around the corner of the banquet hall. I hoped her search for a parking space didn't lead her into the next county.

Snowflakes gathered on the hood of my poufy winter coat as I stomped my feet and rubbed my mittened hands together. Spring couldn't come soon enough for me. I'd had enough snow for this winter.

"Hey, Sam, need any help?"

I turned and saw Marybeth Higgins, a fellow Loopy Lady. The Loopy Ladies is a rug hooking group that meets Monday mornings at The Ewe and Me. We affectionately shortened the name to The Ewe. It was a craft store specializing in rug hooking and all the necessary related supplies, especially wool. Lucy owned it along with her husband Ralph. Like me, Marybeth struggled with her own tote filled with rug hooking wares.

I smiled and shook my head. "Thanks for the offer, but I think you've got as much to schlep in as I do. Candie, I hope, is out back parking Precious. Could you save a seat for us, though? Lucy has a big turnout for her first hook-in."

"No problem. I think Lucy said she expected about one hundred hookers." Marybeth giggled at the shortened name we fellow rug hookers used to refer to ourselves. She leaned towards me and whispered, "I understand Hilda Pratt plans to come."

I rolled my eyes. Hilda was a big thorn in Lucy's side and, according to gossip, a thief. Rumors had swirled amongst the rug hooking community that she'd copied Lucy's rug patterns to sell as her own on the internet. This was not a big deal to some, but the designs Lucy drew up on a piece of linen made up a big part of her income.

"Should make for an interesting day. Here comes Candie. I'll catch up with you inside." I held the glass door to the banquet hall open for Marybeth so she could scoot inside.

I had decided to wait by the entryway for my cousin. I knew she'd only get grumpier if I were settled inside, where I would be snug and warm. This was a day for laughter, good friends, and spending money at the vendors who displayed their new rug hooking patterns and wool. Oh, yes, especially spending money.

Candie stomped her feet and blew on her hands. "The next time we're taking a taxi so the driver can drop us and our belongings off at the door. I finally found a parking space down the street. It's colder than a witch's tits in a brass bra." Candie leaned down and scooped up the large hand-woven bag that contained her rug hooking equipment.

I grabbed the big red canvas bag that held my rug hooking. "Stop exaggerating. It's March. What do you expect? And Memaw would have washed your mouth out with soap if she knew you'd said such a thing." Our Memaw Parker had raised Candie after her parents died in a car accident. Since I was an only child and Candie and I are the same age, my parents had shipped me off every summer to keep her company. Every year, I hadn't been able to wait until the last day of school. I was excited because for three months my cousin and I would run barefoot through the fields of our grandparents' farm in Hainted Holler, Tennessee.

I shifted my brown C–patterned Coach bag up my arm and pulled open the heavy glass door once again. The sound of gossipy hookers filled the cavernous room and bombarded my ears. I stood on tip toe and craned my neck. As I glanced around the room for the Loopy Lady's table. Marybeth saw my stork pose and waved us over.

"Excuse me, sorry, pardon me." I tried not to jab anyone with my bag as I snaked my way across the room crowded with tables and chairs.

"Hi everyone." I dropped my bag on a chair. Candie claimed the one next to me. Eleven of us sat grouped around the table. We ranged in age from eightyish Gladys O'Malley (she'd never reveal her true age) to Susan Mayfield and Marybeth Higgins, both in their thirties. Susan was a young mother who, along with her husband, Brian, owned the best Italian restaurant in Wings Falls, Momma Mia's. Marybeth, one of the quieter members of the group, was a nurse at the town's local hospital— Wings Falls Hospital. She worked the night shift. How she could be so lively after working all night was a wonder to me. Candie and I rested in the middle in our midfifties, and if I didn't get my nightly eight hours, my wagon was dragging.

"What a great turnout for Lucy's first hook-in." I turned to survey the crowd. Ladies sat on folding chairs, either bent over their hooking frames, talking to fellow hookers, or perused the vendors that lined the walls of the banquet hall. Heads nodded in agreement around our table, except for Patsy Ikeda's. She busied herself over her hooking and tried to ignore me. I think she was still miffed at me because I had added her to my suspect list in a murder that I had helped solve last August. Heck, it wasn't my fault the victim had blackmailed her. She tolerated me. I hoped time would heal things between us, as I liked her.

"Oh, a goodie bag." Candie waved a small burlap bag tied with a strip of wool in the air. A thank-you gift from Lucy for all who attended her hook-in sat at each person's place.

Candie undid her bag and dumped the contents on the table. "How cute is this?" She held up a small wooden pin fashioned into the shape of a hook for rug hooking. I suspected Lucy's husband, Ralph, had made them. A retired shop teacher, he carved wooden pins as a hobby. His pins might range from Christmas trees to Easter bunnies or, my favorite, Halloween pumpkins. He displayed them in their store at the check-out counter. They made a great impulse buy when customers paid for their purchases. Along with the pin, an assortment of HERSHEY'S Kisses and a small pad of paper tumbled onto the table. I thumbed through the tablet and noticed The Ewe logo, its address, phone number, and website printed across the top of each page.

I set the tablet on the table next to the candy. "Great advertising." I hitched my purse up my arm. "I'm going to say hi to Lucy and check out the vendors. I need more wool." My comment elicited laughs from around the table. Rug hookers often succumbed to being woolaholics. We never owned enough wool or patterns. Candie claimed it was a disease that knew no cure. I wholeheartedly agreed with her. She said we should form a group and call it WA—Woolaholics Anonymous—but I didn't think too many of us could resist the urge to buy wool for very long. It was a given that we'd all fall off the wagon, sooner rather than later.

As I weaved my way through the crowded hall, I stopped to say hi to ladies I had met at previous hook-ins.

Hooking was a friendly community, populated mostly by women. Every so often a man braved our ranks, but they were few and far between. I oohed and aahed over the designs stretched over the various hooking frames I passed on my way to Lucy's vending area, an alcove tucked into the corner of the banquet hall. My mind's eye pictured bolts of wool spread out on tables with patterns hanging from racks lining the room. I knew I should curb my wool habit. It was eating into my other passion, designer handbags. I needed to find a way to feed each obsession. Hopefully, my new children's book, *Porkchop, the Wonder Dog,* about to debut in a couple of months, would rake in enough money to support both passions in style. One could always dream.

"How dare you accuse me of stealing your pattern ideas and selling them."

"Hilda, I can surf the internet like anyone else. I've seen my patterns for sale on eBay and Etsy, and they weren't posted by me."

I screeched to a halt. I hesitated to enter Lucy's vending space. It was obvious Lucy was in the midst of an argument with Hilda. I held my breath and hugged the wall outside the small nook. I didn't want to intrude on their heated discussion—or, should I say, argument.

"Why would you think they are your patterns?" Hilda asked.

"As they say, if the shoe fits…" Lucy replied.

"Why I never!" Hilda screeched.

"No, Hilda, I don't think you ever did," Lucy said.

I couldn't help myself. I laughed out loud. I was tempted to peek around the corner and see if Hilda was as puffed up as I imagined.

"Lucy Foster, you better not spread any lies about me and your patterns, or you'll be sorry." Hilda stomped out of Lucy's vending area.

"No, Hilda, if I discover any more of my patterns on eBay, you'll be the sorry one," Lucy called after her retreating large form. As Hilda stormed out of Lucy's vending area, she knocked me into the wall. The bracelet she wore that spelled out the word *Hooker* practically imbedded itself into my arm. I don't think she even noticed me. She resembled an avenging

Viking, big boned and towering up to at least six feet tall. Her face was livid with rage.

I walked into Lucy's space, rubbing the arm Hilda had smashed into the wall. "Phew. What was that all about?" I asked, even though I was already aware of the rumors. The mild-mannered Lucy I knew stood surrounded by her patterns and bolts of woolen fabric, gritting her teeth with her hands clenched into fists at her side.

Lucy growled in frustration. "She makes me so mad. A customer told me Hilda was selling my patterns on eBay. I checked it out, and sure enough, I saw them listed for sale. She goes by the seller name Hilda's Prims. She doesn't even try to disguise her name." Lucy pushed a lock of white hair behind her ear.

I placed an arm across Lucy's shoulder in hopes of giving her some comfort. "Geez, I'm sorry. Can't you do anything about it, like report her to eBay? Take some legal action against her?"

Lucy shrugged. "I'm afraid not. Legally she's within her right to create a pattern similar to mine and sell her knockoff as her own. Even if she wasn't, where am I going to get the money for a lawyer to sue her?" She sighed. "Still, it's wrong. Technically legal but wrong."

And upsetting. I shook my head and groaned. If Hilda stole Lucy's pattern designs, it would mean a big hit to her business's bottom line.

I shook my head. "Oh no."

"Yeah, oh no," Lucy repeated. "Hilda's not only selling copies of my patterns, but at a price I can't compete with. I could wring her neck."

CHAPTER TWO

———

I patted Lucy's back. "By the size of this crowd, I'd say the first annual The Ewe and Me hook-in is a success." I wanted to get Lucy's mind off her encounter with Hilda.

Lucy drew in a large, calming breath and smiled. "Yes, thank heavens. I hope it will be a big boost to my business."

Her statement caused me to frown. "Is the store in trouble? Every time I'm at The Ewe, business is hopping."

Lucy straightened her cardigan sweater, a gray knit with two sheep prancing across the front. "The business is holding its own, but Hilda pirating my patterns hasn't helped."

I nodded. My brown curls bounced around my shoulders. "I'm sure it doesn't, but word will get out about Hilda's antics and your loyal customers won't buy her patterns."

"I hope so. I'd hate to take drastic measures to stop her," Lucy said between clenched teeth.

My eyes rounded at the determined expression on her usually mild-mannered face.

"It will all work out, you'll see. Now show me The Ewe's new wool all the Loopy Ladies are raving about," I said, trying to diffuse the situation.

Lucy walked over to a table covered with wool. She pulled a large bag out from underneath it. "Speaking of patterns, I drew up the pattern you wanted of Porkchop. I hope you like the colors I put together to hook it. You said you wanted red for the background."

I clapped my hands together and let out a happy squeal. Porkchop was my six-year-old dachshund and star of my children's book, *Porkchop, the Wonder Dog.* Last week, I had given a picture of him to Lucy and asked her if she could transfer his likeness onto a backing so I could immortalize my pup on a rug. I'd pictured a deep red for the background with a mustardy-yellow border. I reached into the shopping bag and pulled out the pattern. Tears gathered in my eyes as I spread the pattern out on the table and ran my fingers over his image. "Oh, Lucy. You've captured him perfectly. And this wool you've put together for his body matches him perfectly. I can't wait to start hooking him." I ran my hand over the varying shades of reddish-brown wool she had included with the pattern.

Lucy smiled and hugged me. "He's a special pup. I'm so happy you like what I've done."

*　*　*

"You certainly fed my wool habit." Ten minutes later, a shopping bag stuffed with wool and my pattern of Porkchop, dangled from my arm. I shoved a much slimmer wallet into my purse.

Lucy's husband, Ralph, walked into the booth. "I salted the path to the door again. We don't want any hookers to fall on their way into the banquet hall."

Lucy smiled up at him. At six feet, he towered over Lucy's five foot two inches.

"That nervy Hilda Pratt stopped in the booth, but I gave her a piece of my mind." Lucy related her encounter with Hilda to Ralph.

He pulled her into a hug against his tall frame. "Don't worry your pretty little head about her. She'll get her comeuppance one of these days."

Lucy balled her hands into fists. "I hope sooner rather than later."

Ralph bent and placed a kiss on Lucy's forehead. "All will work out."

His reply startled me. What did he know about Hilda that we didn't? Still, in my mind, they shared the perfect love, married forty-five years. Once upon a time, I thought I did, until I had discovered my ex mingling limbs with the secretary of the business we co-owned, the Do Drop Inn Funeral Parlor.

I yanked myself out of those unpleasant memories. Today was a day to have fun, shake off the end of the winter blues, and enjoy the company of fellow hookers. It was a day for inspiration, too. Observing other hookers' works in progress always got my creative juices flowing. With those thoughts in mind, I said goodbye to Lucy and Ralph and set off to circulate around the room. I wanted to get a closer look at what was on everyone's frame and, of course, visit the other vendors at the hook-in.

Such eye candy—lengths of hand-dyed wool, patterns with primitive scenes that ranged from Santas to pumpkins and, of course a love of mine, crows, and much more lined the walls. I longed to buy something from each of the vendors' booths I wandered into. Only the thought of my now depleted wallet and this month's electric bill that sat on my kitchen counter restrained me.

"Oh, Hilda, what a fabulous pattern. I love how you intertwined the flowers around the hearts."

My ears perked up. I turned and noticed that I stood next to Hilda's table. Her friends exclaimed over what I assumed was her latest creation. I peeked over the shoulder of one of the ladies clustered around her and spied the object of their admiration. I couldn't help myself. A loud gasp escaped my lips.

Five heads swiveled my way. Heat flushed my face. If I gazed into a mirror right then, my face would probably be glowing as red as Santa's rosy cheeks.

"Ummm," I stammered. "What a beautiful pattern. Lucy did a great job designing it, didn't she?"

"What do you mean? It's one of Hilda's originals." Mari Adams, a fast friend of Hilda, sprang to her defense. Like most people, the top of Mari's gray-streaked brown head barely reached Hilda's shoulder. I would bet that if Hilda said "Jump!" Mari would ask "How high?"

The other ladies nodded in agreement. Hilda used her height and broad build to her advantage by intimidating people into faithful followers.

I wasn't one to easily back down from a potentially nasty situation. I threw back my shoulders and said, "Sorry to disagree with you, but I sat hooking in The Ewe while Lucy designed it. She asked me my opinion of the pattern while it lay on her drafting table."

The ladies who were gathered around Hilda resembled the fish in my childhood aquarium at feeding time. Their mouths gaped open, as they tried to suck in food flakes.

Hilda balled up the pattern and stuffed it into a large bag that rested on the chair next to her. "There's nothing new in the design world. Everything has already been done. So, my design has a slight resemblance to Lucy's. No big deal. Come on, ladies. Let's go check out the vendors." With a wave of her large hand, Hilda motioned for her minions to follow her.

I watched them in amazement. The group trailed behind Hilda like puppies lured with a tasty bone. From the glimpse I had caught of the pattern, Lucy was correct. Hilda had copied her patterns. What Lucy and Ralph would do about it, I could only imagine. From what they'd said in their booth, they were determined to put an end to Hilda's thievery. I wasn't going to get involved.

I continued my journey around the room and stopped on my circuit, frequently, to admire and comment on various hookers' rugs that caught my eye. Finally, I arrived back at the Loopy Ladies' table.

I sat in my chair and reached for my hooking.

Candie glanced up from her rug. "What took you so long? I noticed you at Hilda's table. She acted rather upset with you. What did you say to get her so agitated?"

Ten pairs of eyes gazed at me. My fellow Loopy Ladies waited for my answer. I related the events of my stop at Lucy's booth, the conversation I had overheard and what I saw when I stopped by Hilda's table. I also mentioned that she'd claimed one of Lucy's patterns as her own.

"You're right," Anita Plum said. "I was at The Ewe the day Lucy designed that pattern, too. I think she asked all of us our opinion of her design." Anita swore that the mindless pulling of wool loops kept her sane while she dealt with her twin teenage daughters.

Helen Garber peered over the bright orange frames of her glasses. "Lucy values our opinion. And that Mari Adams—I never did understand why she sucked up to Hilda the way she did. I mean, if a woman had stolen my husband, I can't say I'd be her bosom buddy the way she is with Hilda." Helen was one of the more outspoken members of our group and didn't mince her words.

Heads nodded around the table.

I raised my eyebrows. "Hilda stole Mari's husband?"

"Honestly, Sam, what rock have you been living under?" Helen shook her head. Her bright, red-dyed hair was pulled back in a French twist. Helen might be in her midsixties, but she fought aging with every bright outfit she wore, and today was no exception. She had paired an oversize top that matched the color of her hair with flowing orange pants.

I never got involved in the town gossip. My own divorce had provided enough fuel for the town gossips to last me a lifetime.

"Poor Mari. Tied down with two young ones. Hilda had flaunted herself in front of Mari's husband, and zap, before you knew it, he became husband number two for Hilda. The bum left Mari to raise her two boys by herself."

Heads around the table glanced up from their hooking frames and nodded at Helen's statement.

"It'd be a cold day at the equator before I'd cozy up to any woman who stole my husband." Candie poked the air with her rug hook for emphasis.

I agreed with my cousin. I might be cordial to my ex's wife, but only because we needed to maintain a working relationship. Plus, they had adorable twin boys. But friendly? Was not going to happen.

I settled into my seat and picked up my rug hook. I began to pull loops of red, white, and blue wool on a pattern for a table runner of stars and circles. When finished, I planned to drape it across the top of the trunk in front of my sofa, for the summer's patriotic holidays.

The conversation around the table turned to children and grandchildren. I couldn't claim having had either, so I listened more than contributed. Until Cookie Harrington, the new receptionist at the Wings Falls Animal Hospital (the former receptionist was arrested last fall for murder—but that was a whole different story), asked me about Porkchop.

Thoughts of my fur baby brought a smile to my lips. "Fine. He's due for his annual check-up soon, so I need to call and set one up to make sure he has all his shots. My editor wants him to join me when I do book signings. He's such a ham already that I can't imagine how he'll act when he's surrounded by his fans."

The ladies laughed. They knew how my pup loved attention since he often accompanied me to The Ewe, where he received lots of pats and the occasional doggie treat. Ralph always had a rawhide bone ready for his favorite shop dog.

"In fact, let me show you what Lucy drew up for me." I pulled the pattern of Porkchop out of the paper bag and held it up for all the ladies to see.

"Is that the next pattern going on your frame?" Gladys asked. Bright green curls bounced about her head. I smiled. Gladys changed her hair color according to the latest celebration. This month she had tinted it green for Saint Patrick's Day. The coming Easter season called for a pink hue. The Fourth of July saw red and blue streaks mingled in her hair.

"Definitely. When it's finished, I might even bring it with me when I do book signings. Porkchop can lie on it while his fans ooh and aah over him." This brought another round of laughter from the ladies.

I laid my hook on the table. "I think my morning cup of coffee is calling. Anyone know where the ladies' room is?" I had never been in this banquet hall before.

Candie swiveled in her chair and pointed to the rear of the room. "Over there, in the back."

I raised an eyebrow. How did she know the bathroom's location?

She must have noticed the quizzical expression on my face. "I've been here before for awards dinners with Mark." Mark Hogan was the mayor of Wings Falls and Candie's on again-off again boyfriend. I suspected he'd like to be more on than off. With eleven engagements in her past, Candie suffered from a slight commitment problem. She'd sworn off engagements for life. If a fellow managed to wrangle a second date from her, he was lucky. I suspected Mark had breached the two-date maximum Candie imposed. Candie worked as Mark's part-time secretary. Wings Falls didn't have the budget to hire her full-time. Which suited her fine. It gave her time to write her romance novels.

"Be back in a minute," I said and pushed away from the table.

At least, I thought a simple trip to the ladies' room would take only a few minutes. I was dead wrong.

CHAPTER THREE

———

"I'll be right behind you. I want to finish this row." Candie pointed her hook at her pattern. The design was adapted from an antique rug with a momma duck that swam in a pond with her three babies.

It wasn't like I couldn't go to the bathroom without my cousin trailing along, but I think she wanted to talk to me about the Lucy/Hilda incident without prying Loopy Lady ears. My brow creased. Did she know something the rest of the group didn't?

I pushed open the door to the ladies' room. Like most institutional buildings, it was utilitarian at best. The cinderblock walls were painted gray and pink with the standard porcelain sinks lining one wall. Metal stalls enclosed the johns, but the main thing—it was clean. A folding chair, so dented I thought a fire engine might have run over it a few times, sat in a corner. Pull-up air fresheners rested on the sinks. They gave the room a hint of a floral aroma. The distinct smell of vomit tainted that floral scent. The sound of retching came from behind a stall door.

I walked over to the closed stall door and called out, "Can I help you?"

A faint, garbled reply answered me. "Please, I think I'm dying."

I pressed on the unlatched door. An ashen-faced Hilda Pratt leaned over the toilet. She turned towards me. Vomit stained the front of her sweater. Her trembling arms reached out to me. I grasped her hand and led her out of the stall towards the chair. I needed to get her into the main part of the room where I could better help her.

"Have a seat. I'm going to soak some paper towels and place them across your forehead. The cool towels should make you feel better." I don't know why I thought they would cure what ailed her, but I needed to do something, and soaking paper towels was all I could come up with other than going into full panic mode. I'm lousy in a crisis.

Hilda nodded. I sprang into action and ran over to the sink. I pulled a handful of paper towels from the dispenser hanging over the sink, wet them under the faucet, then hurried back to her.

"Here." I placed a towel on her sweating forehead.

Her face had turned a deathly white. A dark shade of bluish-purple tinted her lips. Panic snaked through my body. Where was someone, anyone, when you needed them? Usually, the most visited place in a building—this ladies' room stood as empty as a tomb. The serious hookers were probably spending money at the vendors. A pit stop could wait until the last possible moment.

By the sweat pouring down Hilda's face and her ruddy cheeks, now the color of the Pillsbury Dough Boy, "empty as a tomb" was a poor choice of words. Her hands trembled as she raked them through her gray hair, causing it to stand out like a porcupine's quills. Her right wrist was red and scratched.

"Hilda, I have to go get you some help."

She grabbed my hand. For someone so obviously ill, her hands that trembled a moment ago now gripped mine like a steel vise. "No," she rasped, her voice a faint whisper. "I don't want to die alone."

I knelt beside her. "Now, don't talk such nonsense. You're going to be fine, but you need medical attention."

She shook her head vigorously, then clutched her throat with one of her broad hands.

I knew I had to ignore her plea. I stood and turned to get her the help she needed.

Before I took two steps towards the door, a thump sounded behind me. I spun around and saw Hilda crumpled on the floor. Her glassy eyes stared up at the ceiling.

I raced over and placed two fingers gingerly on her neck then silently prayed, "Please, Lord, let there be a pulse." But I felt nothing, not even a blip.

The bathroom door swung open. "Sam, what's taking you so long?" Candie gasped. "What in God's green pea garden is happening?" She rushed over and knelt beside Hilda.

She looked at Hilda then me. "Is she?" Her violet eyes pleaded for a "no" answer. I regretted that I couldn't give her what she wanted.

I shook my head and related to her what had happened from the time I had entered the bathroom to do my business— which, by the way, I still needed to do. But now wasn't the right time to drop my Fruit of the Looms, not with a dead body right outside the stalls.

"Do you have your cell phone? We need to call 9-1-1."

My cousin groaned. She knew why I couldn't place the call. Unlike most people, my cell phone was one of those you must buy minutes for. It usually hovered around three minutes or less, and I forgot to reload it this month.

Candie dug into the pocket of her skirt. She extracted her bejeweled cell phone and punched in the universal help number. True, we were in the banquet room of the firehouse, but the rescue squad was housed in another building two blocks away.

Candie explained our situation to the dispatcher then slid her phone back into the pocket of her flowing skirt. "The dispatcher said they'll be right here. Shouldn't we do CPR or something?"

I placed my fingers on Hilda's neck again and prayed for a pulse but couldn't find one. I jerked my head towards the bathroom door. "Oh, no! Candie, listen!" Panic filled me. The sound of voices approaching the bathroom filtered through the door. Obviously, other hookers' morning coffees had called them, too. "We can't let anyone in here."

Candie strode over to the door. She inched it open and peeked outside. "Sorry, ladies, the toilets have overflowed. It's a real mess in here. You wouldn't want to ruin your shoes."

A skinny hooker with heavily frosted hair said, "What am I going to do? I can't wait much longer. My kidneys will burst." She turned to the group of ladies lined up behind her. "I didn't dare get out of line at Lucy's booth. She offered such good bargains on dyed wool."

The other ladies murmured in agreement. Feeding their wool addiction trumped any call of nature.

Candie nodded. "I understand. Hey, why not commandeer the men's room? Ralph is the only male here, so no one will be using it."

A smile creased the hooker's wrinkled face. "Ohhh, I was always curious what the inside of a men's room looks like."

The ladies giggled as if on a grand adventure and marched down the hall to the men's room.

Candie walked over to the paper towel dispenser and yanked out a fistful of towels.

She knelt beside me. "What are you doing?" I asked.

"I'm going to cover up her face. Her eyes staring up at the ceiling is creeping me out."

I brushed her hand away. "Stop. We can't touch anything until the EMTs and police come."

Candie pouted. "Oh, all right." She deposited the towels in the trash can next to the sink. "Do you think Hank will answer the call?"

I sent a silent prayer to heaven and hoped my somewhat boyfriend, Hank Johnson, detective with the Wings Falls Police, wasn't the officer who responded to the call. I would have loved to see him, but not under these circumstances. A murder was how we met last August when I discovered another dead body. At least this wasn't a murder, or so I hoped.

"He's off today. He's taking Nina to have her nails trimmed." Nina was Hank's adorable bulldog and my dog's BFF. They had bonded at first sight. "In fact, we're having dinner tonight at the new restaurant Marybeth Higgins' brother opened on Main Street, The Smiling Pig. Do you and Mark want to join us?" I asked.

Candie nodded. "Sure, we haven't planned anything special. And I hear they serve up fantastic barbeque."

Geez, what was I thinking, making inane conversation over a dead body, but what do you talk about while waiting for the police and rescue squad to arrive?

Candie stared down at Hilda who laid on the cold tile floor of the bathroom. "Do you think we should put something under Hilda's head to make her more comfortable?"

If the situation wasn't so tragic, I would have laughed out loud. "I don't think she cares much right now."

"Yes, but Memaw would have said we weren't being very hospitable."

I agreed with Candie. Our Memaw Parker would probably have passed around butter cookies and sweet tea about now. She'd make sure everyone, even the deceased, was served according to proper Southern hospitality.

Candie crossed her arms over her ample chest. "What do you think happened to her?"

"I know she suffered from allergies to certain foods. I attended a class on hooking in monochromatic colors last year. I had planned to hook a rug for the top of the sweater chest in my bedroom. She was in the class too. Come lunchtime, all she did was complain that she couldn't eat half of what was on the buffet line because the food would cause her to break out in a rash."

"I remember when you took that class. The flowers in your rug were beautiful. Who'd have thought there were so many different shades of white. But I can't imagine, by the size of Hilda, she'd be allergic to any food."

"Candie!" I chided. "Be kind. She's dead at our feet."

She had the good grace to blush. "You're right. Memaw would have scolded me for saying such an unkind thing. But wouldn't Hilda have carried an EpiPen with her if she was so allergic to food?"

"Since you mentioned it, I would think so, but in that class, she never said anything about needing one. Then again, she collapsed pretty fast. Listen, I hear sirens." I glanced at my Timex watch, a present from my parents when I graduated from Cornell. It felt like an hour had passed and not the five minutes since Candie had placed the 9-1-1 call.

The bathroom door burst open. I closed my eyes and groaned. I thought today was his day off.

"Sam?" he said. "What are you doing here?"

A weak smile curved my lips. I returned his greeting with a feeble waggle of my fingers.

Candie whispered in my ear, "Do you think you should cancel tonight's dinner reservation?"

Judging by the frown that creased Hank's forehead, I said, "Yep."

CHAPTER FOUR

———

Even though Hank wasn't thrilled to discover me with another dead body, he still smiled his crooked grin at me. My fingers itched to brush back the lock of curly brown hair constantly falling over his forehead. Despite this dire predicament, my insides quivered at the sight of him.

"Move back, ladies. Let law enforcement through. Make way for the medics."

Oh no. Canceling dinner reservations was the least of my problems. That voice belonged to my kindergarten nemesis, Sergeant Joe Peters. He and I had been on the outs since we were five years old. It wasn't my fault he peed in the sandbox way back then. So I had told the playground attendant. Big deal. I mean, who would want to play in pee-soaked sand?

Joe—or as he became known in grade school by his hated nickname, Sandy—strode to a halt a foot in front of me. If he thought invading my personal space would intimidate me, he was wrong, dead wrong. Oops. Maybe another poor choice of words.

Peters tapped his chin. "Hmm, involved in another death, Ms. Davies?"

I inhaled a deep breath. Sergeant Peters must have overdosed on his Old Spice cologne this morning.

I stepped back a foot and waved a hand in front of my face then exhaled. "Sandy, I mean Sergeant Peters. Contrary to what you might think, I had nothing to do with Hilda's death."

Joe Peters grunted, "We'll see."

I glanced in Hank's direction and hoped for some help, but he stood over Hilda's body talking with the EMTs who crowded into the bathroom.

"If you're not involved, tell me why you happen to be here with this dead woman?" Joe Peters pulled a pad of paper out of his gray uniform shirt pocket. He gripped a pencil in his beefy hand, ready to jot down my statement.

I groaned inwardly. I knew from last August's experience of stumbling onto a dead person this would be the first of many times I would recite the events that took place from the moment I entered the ladies' room and discovered Hilda worshiping the porcelain god.

Joe furrowed his dark unibrow at me. "You said you came in here to go to the bathroom. Why didn't you go before you left home? If memory serves me correctly, you live only a few miles from here. Isn't it a little soon after you left your house to have a call of nature?"

Exasperated, my knuckles turned white from clenching them so hard. I had to either put up with the white knuckles or punch the idiot in his chest, but I'd probably do more harm to my hand when I punched his bulletproof vest.

"Sandy, you obviously don't know the workings of women our age. If a bathroom is nearby, nature calls us." I'd said enough, so I turned on my heels and marched over to Candie, who stood by the bathroom door.

"Sergeant Peters to you," he called after me.

"Yeah, yeah," I mumbled under my breath.

"Whoa." Candie caught me by the arms before I plowed into her.

I let out a shaky breath. Joe Peters rattled me. "The jerk." I pointed a shaking finger at him. "He thinks I have something to do with Hilda's death."

"What!" Candie screeched. "Is he nuts? I'm going to give him a piece of my mind. He'll find out what happens when he messes with us Parkers."

I grabbed Candie's arm to restrain her. A taste of her Southern wrath was not a pretty sight even on a warm sunny day, let alone a gloomy winter one like today.

"It's okay. Hank will sort things out, and the medical examiner will discover what Hilda was allergic to and caused her to have such a reaction."

"Like I said before, don't you think it's odd she didn't carry her EpiPen with her at all times, especially if she was so allergic to food?" Candie asked.

I shook my head. "I don't know."

Candie frowned at me.

"I mean, she was only going to the bathroom after all. You know I get migraines, but I don't carry my pain meds with me to the bathroom." I stood next to Candie and watched Hank converse with the EMTs. By the frown marring his handsome face, he didn't look too pleased with what they said.

"Oh, for heaven's sake, you're not going to drop dead if you don't have your migraine pills on you." Candie pulled a HERSHEY'S Kiss out of the pocket of her voluminous peasant skirt. She pealed the silver foil wrapper off the candy and popped it into her mouth. Geez, my cousin could make eating a piece of chocolate sexy. I thought one of the young emergency techs crowded in with us would have heart palpitations as he eyed her licking the chocolate from her lips.

"Obviously, you've never suffered from migraines, or you wouldn't say such a thing. When I'm in the throes of one of my doozie headaches, I think I'd welcome the relief of eternal rest to the pain shooting around my brain."

Candie shook her head and rolled her eyes at me.

I held out my hand. "Here, hand over a Kiss. I need something sweet to take the sour taste of death out of my mouth."

She rooted in her pocket and pulled out another candy.

* * *

I glanced at my watch and blinked. Over an hour had passed since I'd entered the ladies' room. "How much longer will we be here? Hank is still talking with EMTs and Joe Peters." The medics were loading Hilda's body onto a gurney. I wondered if that was a sign the body was about to be transferred to the hospital for the medical examiner's attention.

"Why don't you ask Hank if we can leave or at least go back to our table?" Candie asked around another piece of chocolate. She certainly wasn't letting the contents of her goodie bag go to waste.

"All right," I said. I caught Hank's eye and crooked a finger to motion him over.

"Are you okay?" he asked, striding up to me.

My breath hitched in my throat as it always did when he stood next to me. I still couldn't believe I was dating this incredibly kind man, who also happened to be outstandingly handsome.

I longed to touch the shadow of a beard that darkened his cheeks and jaw. The curl of brown hair that fell onto his forehead still begged for my attention. All I wanted to do was lay my head on his chest and have him make this whole nightmare go away. But this wasn't the time or place.

"I'm fine, but do you think Candie and I could go back to our table? I've answered all of Joe's questions." I glanced over at Sergeant Peters, who stood next to Hilda's body. He was deep in conversation with the medics and pointed to Hilda's neck.

"Sure. I don't know why not, but no one will be allowed to leave the hook-in soon. Everyone needs to be questioned— names, contact information," Hank replied.

"Detective Johnson, come here. Look at this," Joe called from across the room.

"Sorry, I have got to go." Hank reached over and squeezed my hand.

I about melted into my snow boots. Even in these dire circumstances, he showed his concern about how I felt. My life had lacked his kind of tenderness for far too long. It was as if I had wandered in a desert dying of thirst and he offered me life-giving water. Guess that said a lot about how my ex had treated me.

Candie and I saw no need for us to remain in the ladies' room, so we turned to leave.

"Where do you think you're going?" Joe shouted at our backs.

I spun on my heels and, with my sweetest voice, ground out between clenched teeth, "Back to our table, Sandy. Detective Johnson gave us permission to leave."

Red flushed his face. "Make sure you don't leave the building. It's mighty strange that you were present at Ms. Pratt's death."

I opened my mouth to reply, but Candie tugged on my arm to stop me. "Do you have a death wish or something? You know Joe hates being called Sandy. He would lock you up and throw away the key if he could. Come on. Let's go back to our table. Maybe we'll get a little hooking done." She whipped open the door and pushed me through.

"Excuse me, excuse me," I repeated as I tried to nudge my way through the crowd of ladies gathered outside the bathroom door.

Why did a tragedy bring out the ghoul in people? Questions of "What did you see?" and "How did Hilda look?" and "Did blood cover the bathroom floor?" followed me to my table.

I shook my head in disbelief. "How can people be so insensitive?"

Candie shrugged her shoulders. "I think they're just relieved it isn't them going out of here feet first on a gurney."

I settled into the seat I had vacated what felt like hours ago. "I guess you're right. I'm sure when Hilda woke up this morning, she didn't think she'd be pulling her last loop today."

Candie pointed at my sweater. "Sam, hush. What's hanging off your sleeve?"

I glanced in the direction she had pointed. I saw a pin shaped like a rug-hooking hook, similar to the ones Ralph had carved for our goodie bag. I carefully lifted it off my sweater. I noticed something odd about this one. The slim metal pin part of the hook was red. Bloodred.

CHAPTER FIVE

———

All eyes swiveled toward my sleeve as I gingerly pulled the pin off my sweater.

Gladys O'Malley leaned forward in her chair. Her tight, green-dyed curls bounced about her head. Because she hated to wear her bifocals, she squinted at the pin. She pointed at it with one of her gnarled fingers. "Is that blood covering the pin?"

I gasped and dropped the pin on the table in front of me.

Questions tumbled from the Loopy Ladies. Of course, Helen Garber was the first to ask, "Was it Hilda's pin? Is that her blood?"

Jane Burrows, our town librarian, pushed tortoiseshell-rimmed glasses up her nose and chimed in, "Why was it on your sweater? Did you stick her with it?"

At the last question, Candie's face turned beet red. She exploded, "How can you ask such a question, Jane? You all know Sam. She is kind and caring. She tried to help Hilda. She would do the same for any of you if you became ill."

The ladies all looked properly chastised as they picked up their hooks and busied themselves with their projects.

I closed my eyes and silently willed the pin to disappear. I opened them and knew that the hooking gods had not granted my wish. It still lay on the table in front of me. I hesitated to touch the pin, although I didn't know what difference it would make now since my fingerprints were smeared on it. I reached for my hook and poked at the pin. Did I think my hook was a magic wand and if I jabbed the pin it would vanish? If so, my magic had run out. The pin didn't go anywhere. It lay on the table in all its bloodred glory as if to say, "Wait until Joe Peters sees this."

Candie leaned towards me and whispered, "How *do* you think the pin got stuck to your sweater?"

My brow creased in thought. My cousin had asked the question of the hour, and I needed an answer. I knew the sergeant would ask me the same thing, and I had to come up with a good one if I didn't want to leave the hook-in wearing a new set of bracelets, the kind issued by the Wings Falls Police Department for all their murder suspects. I could only imagine the grin on Joe Peters' face as he snapped them closed and, I bet, a little tighter than necessary. My wrists ached at the thought.

"Honestly, Candie, I don't know. Maybe it snagged onto my sweater when she collapsed into my arms." I swallowed hard. Would Peters buy my story? Something told me the answer was a big fat no.

"Well, it wouldn't surprise me one little bit if they found something more to Hilda's death than meets the eye."

My gaze snapped to Roberta Holden, who sat across the table from me. "What do you mean?" I asked.

Roberta peered at me over the top of her cherry-red half glasses. A long-time member of our group and a very accomplished hooker, she often helped Lucy at The Ewe. She taught lessons to newbie hookers.

Roberta ran a hand through her blonde curls then pulled at the neck of her blouse. "I'm only saying Hilda ruffled more than Lucy's feathers. Why, my Clyde would come home from his barber shop with stories galore about Hilda's antics. You think women gossip, dearie? Men tell more tales by far than we do. They'd climb into Clyde's barber chair and chatter away like magpies on speed."

Heads bobbed around the table in agreement with Roberta. Apparently, Clyde Holden, Roberta's husband, who owned the town's most popular barber shop, was the go-to guy for all the town's gossip. Were my ex and I ever discussed in the confines of his small shop? Especially when he spent late nights mattress dancing with our funeral parlor's secretary? Heat crawled up my neck as I thought of my name as the subject of gossip central.

My own curiosity piqued, I asked, "So, what did Hilda do to upset people?"

Thank heavens, Roberta now commanded the center of attention and, by her grin, loved it, too. Hooks poised in mid-air waiting for Roberta to speak. She pushed a strand of her blonde hair behind her ear, leaned forward, and said in a raspy whisper, "Well, I don't want to spread more gossip..." Heads nodded around the table. That gave her the encouragement she needed to continue. "But, Clyde said, a few years back when Hilda worked at the bank, she offered some risky investment advice. Nothing illegal, mind you, but more than a few people lost money."

"Were you one of her clients?" I asked. Did Roberta have a reason to rejoice over Hilda's death?

"Why, umm, well." Roberta rubbed her hands down the front of her jeans. Her left eye started to twitch. Now why was she suddenly nervous?

She waved her hand to dismiss my question. "It was only a few dollars. Nothing significant. I've lost more playing the slot machines at the racino in Saratoga." With a nervous laugh, she picked up her hook and turned to Jane Burrows. "Jane, if I remember correctly, didn't you take Hilda to court when she served on the town council?"

Jane's hook clattered to the table. If the old saying "if looks could kill" was correct, Roberta would join Hilda on the pathway to heaven or possibly that hot place.

"It's ancient history. No need to drag it up," Jane snapped. "Excuse me, I need to get a cup of coffee. Franny has put a fresh urn out on the buffet table." Jane stuck her hook into her rug pattern of a bowl of poppies then pushed back her chair and stood. The sound of the metal legs scraping on the tile floor of the firehouse sent chills up my spine. She pushed her tortoiseshell glasses to the top of her head, causing her pixie haircut to stand on end. Next, she tugged at the hem of one of the many sweater sets she owned. Today's combo was a Kelly green that she had paired with a pair of crisply ironed khaki slacks. Like Gladys O'Malley's hair color choice, Jane often spiced up her wardrobe with sweater sets to match certain occasions or holidays. The green sweater set, I surmised, like Gladys's green hair, was for Saint Patrick's Day. With her back ramrod straight, she marched away from our table towards the coffee.

My gaze followed Jane over to the buffet, where Franny Goodway, who owned the best Southern-style restaurant in the north country, Sweetie Pie's Café, had placed some delicious muffins on the buffet table to go with a fresh urn of coffee. In my opinion, it looked like a few of the Loopy Ladies had some "history" with Hilda. What made Jane so jittery about Roberta's question?

"She has some nerve. Don't let her Goody-Two-Shoes librarian act fool you," Roberta said, jabbing her hook into her rug pattern.

"*Did* Jane sue Hilda when she served on town council?" I asked, confused about the question.

"Don't you remember about five years ago a fellow bought the old mini golf course down the road from her home?" Roberta asked. My question must have relaxed her some, as she hooked more calmly now.

I groaned inwardly. Was I so unaware of what was going on around me when I went through my divorce? I shrugged. "Guess I had been a little preoccupied at the time." The understatement of the century.

Candie coughed. I glanced at her. Her eyes were focused on her project. I detected a faint smile twitch the corners of her lips and kicked her under the table.

"Ouch!" She glared at me and rubbed her shin.

"So, what caused Jane to sue Hilda?" I asked, my rug hooking abandoned and my full attention on Roberta. I wasn't the only one who waited for her answer. All the other Loopy Ladies watched Roberta intently for her to speak.

Roberta preened under all the attention. She sat up straighter and thrust her already massive breasts out. I feared her straining blouse buttons would pop.

"As you all know, I write a column for the *Senior Chatter*, the newsletter published by the Wings Falls Senior Center." Heads nodded at Roberta's pronouncement. "I cover all the town council meetings so our older citizens are informed about what happens in City Hall. We don't want any of those politicians to try to pull anything over on us. We may be a little advanced in age, but that doesn't mean we don't want to know about any of their shenanigans."

Candie cleared her throat and aimed dagger eyes towards Roberta.

"Oh, I don't mean Mark." Roberta had the decency to blush. "We all know he's as honest as they come."

Once again, heads bobbed in agreement.

"What does that have to do with Jane?" I wanted to hear this story before the spring thaw began.

"I'll get to it. Be patient."

I heaved a sigh and settled back in my seat. Would the first robins of spring chirp outside the banquet hall before this story ended?

"So, there I sat with my pad of paper and pencil, ready to take notes, when Hilda addressed her fellow council member. She wanted to introduce a Mr. Farnsdale. She said he was going to propose a plan to benefit all of Wings Falls and lower the town's taxes. Well, of course, everyone's ears perked up. He spun a good tale about how he planned to put in a dirt bike track. He had brought charts and flyers to support all of his claims."

"Oh, I remember him," Gladys piped in. "No better than a snake oil salesman if you ask me."

Anita Plum spoke up. "You're right. My Susie and Sara were only in grade school. He tried to pass the flyers out to kids as they left school. The principal got wind of it, and he was 'escorted' away from the school property."

I shook my head. "That's terrible. How did he even get close to the school?"

"He sort of blended in with all the other parents picking their kids up from school. I was substituting for the art teacher that day. I told my girls to meet me in the art room at dismissal time, but they arrived a little late. Those twins of mine can get easily distracted." Anita rolled her eyes. Her daughters were in their teens now and the reason for several of their parents' gray hairs.

"How were the flyers handed out?" Patsy Ikeda asked.

All rug hooking halted as heads swiveled towards Anita.

"My girls said they forgot I was substituting that day and waited outside for me to pick them up for a few minutes before they remembered to meet me in the art room." Anita shook her head. "He stood on the sidewalk outside the school and passed them out. Believe me, my girls got an ear blistering on the way home from school about taking anything from a stranger."

Chuckles and knowing looks spread around the group. Unfortunately, Candie and I didn't have any child-rearing experience to relate to this.

To move the story along as to why Jane might have a grudge against Hilda Pratt, I prompted, "What does all of this have to do with Jane not liking Hilda?"

"Jane lived next to a defunct mini-golf course." Roberta pulled a strip of orange wool through her pumpkin rug pattern.

"Doesn't she live with her mother in Sunny Hills Condos now?" I asked. Sunny Hills was a nice fifty-five and older development with everything provided, from lawn care to snow shoveling. I glanced out the banquet hall's window. As the snow fell in large flakes, that sounded awfully appealing on a day like this.

"She does, but she could barely scrape the money together to move there. The dirt bike park Mr. Farnsdale proposed made it through the town council on the fast track. As part of the approval process, the council ordered him to put up all kinds of barriers to block the noise from the motorcycles, but he never did. Jane practically gave her house away when she sold it. Who wanted to live next to the din of motorcycles racing every day?"

"What a shame. Wasn't he given regulations about the noise or hours of operation to follow?" I asked, my brow furrowed in thought. Surely there were noise pollution regulations or some ordinances he needed to obey.

"Humph," snorted Helen Garber. I was surprised she had remained silent this long. "He got away with whatever he liked. They even fast-tracked a liquor license for him. Can you imagine mixing motorcycles and booze?"

"So how does this all tie in with Jane and Hilda?" I asked, still not sure of the connection.

Roberta stared at me as if two heads had sprouted from my neck and neither had contained any brains. "Don't you understand? The property value of Jane's house plummeted. She blames Hilda for pushing Mr. Farnsdale's agenda for the dirt bike track. She tried to sue her for damages but didn't get anywhere."

Ah. The light suddenly went on in my brain. So more than a few people weren't exactly fond of Hilda. It was a good thing she died of natural causes. The blood-dipped pin stared up at me.

Or did she?

CHAPTER SIX

———

I groaned and pushed back my chair. I dreaded the confrontation about to happen between Joe Peters and me. I needed to hand the pin over to him as evidence, but I also suspected he would accuse me of tampering with the death scene. He'd already tried to blame a murder on me last year. Fingers crossed, maybe I'd get lucky and be able to give the incriminating object to Hank. He would believe my story on how the pin may have become attached to my sweater. I'd only wanted to go to the bathroom. How was I to know a call of nature would end with my discovering a dying Hilda?

I'm handing in my do-gooder's badge. Next time I come across someone in need of help, I'll turn on my heels and run, not walk away.

With a nod of my head to convince myself, I wrapped the pin in a napkin and stood.

Candie looked up from her hooking. "Where are you going?"

I rolled my eyes. "I'm sure this pin is important, so I'd better return to the ladies' room and give it to Joe or, hopefully, Hank."

Candie coughed, trying to stifle a laugh.

"This isn't funny. A pin with her blood on it will only convince Joe I'm involved. He will accuse me of having something to do with her death. I'll be lucky if the next time you see me isn't visiting day at the county jail. What if Big Bula is my cell mate?" I stared at the napkin-wrapped pin clutched in my hand. "Will you give Porkchop a good home? I know he and Dixie are not the best of friends, but maybe they will grow to like one another." Candie's cat, Dixie, barely tolerated my sweet dog. "Do you think the guards would allow Porkchop to visit me in prison? He is my closest family member."

Candie raised a perfectly shaped eyebrow at me.

"After you, of course," I hastened to add.

"You're silly. Joe has to have more brain cells than to accuse you of anything other than trying to help Hilda in her hour of need." Candie poked the air with her hook to emphasize her words.

"We're talking about Joe Peters here. The man who has held a grudge against me since kindergarten," I said.

"Do you want me to come with you?" Candie placed her hook down on the table and started to rise.

I shook my head. "Thanks, but no thanks."

"Where ya goin'?" Gladys asked. She squinted up at me over her hooking frame.

"I figure I better hand the pin over to Sergeant Peters. I don't know if it is important or not."

I turned in the direction of the ladies' room and set off on my duty-bound mission. A chorus of "good luck"s followed me from my table.

"Thanks." I called over my shoulder. Why did I feel like I was about to climb the steps to a guillotine? Was this how Marie Antoinette had felt on her fateful day?

I scanned the banquet hall as I made my way across the noise-filled room. Busy fingers pulled loops at each table. Conversations stopped when I passed my fellow hookers. Did these ladies think I was involved in Hilda's death? Was I letting my imagination run wild? Sure, a few months ago I'd discovered a dead body, but just like that man, I'd had nothing to do with Hilda's death. She'd become sick and I'd tried to help her. Period. End of conversation. Or so I thought.

"It is awfully strange. Lately, whenever someone dies unexpectedly, Sam is there."

I whipped my head around. Who had uttered those condemning words? I stood next to Hilda's table. Her friends stared up at me.

I gritted my teeth and said, "It so happens it was my misfortune to be in the ladies' room when your fearless leader got sick and died. I did everything I could to help her."

"Right," Mari Adams said.

My eyes snapped to Mari. What did her remark imply?

I sucked in a deep breath and tried to rein in my anger. After all, Mari had lost a good friend.

"I'm sorry for your loss, Mari. I know you and Hilda were close, but I assure you I had nothing to do with Hilda's death."

"If you say so," she replied. She ignored me and rooted through a pile of wool strips that lay before her on the table.

"Yes, I do. I only wanted to help her. I didn't notice any of you in the ladies' room comforting her." If they gave out prizes for keeping one's temper under control, I would have won first prize, hands down.

"Sam, Sam."

I turned in the direction of the voice that called my name. Lucy Foster beckoned me over to her booth.

Her appearance was dreadful. Her soft white hair, which she usually tucked neatly behind her ears in a bob, looked like a windstorm had blown through it. She stood by a table ladened with bolts of wool and wrung her hands while Ralph waited on a customer. I guess even a tragedy couldn't stop a hooker's love of gathering as much wool as possible.

I scurried over to her. "Lucy, what's wrong? I mean, I know Hilda's death is a terrible thing to happen here at your first hook-in, but you didn't have anything to do with it."

Lucy opened her mouth then snapped it shut again. She drew a trembling hand through her hair. Now, I understood why her usually neat-as-a-pin hair stood straight up.

"Come here and sit," I said, edging Lucy over to a folding chair in her booth. "Can I get you a glass of water?" I didn't know what else to do to soothe her growing agitation. Water was the go-to cure-all to calm people down, other than a shot of whiskey, but I didn't think Lucy kept a spare bottle in her booth. I glanced over at Ralph and saw him eyeing us. I shrugged my shoulders up and down to let him know I wanted to help Lucy. He answered me with a nod of his head.

"Please tell me what has you so upset. Did Sergeant Peters say something to you?" My dander rose, big-time. I would wring his beefy neck if he had upset my dear friend.

"No, no, it isn't anything like that. He's been very kind. And especially your gentleman friend, Detective Johnson, although he asked me for a list of the attendees at the hook-in. I couldn't imagine what he'd want it for. But I'm worried about my misunderstanding between Hilda and me earlier in the day. Do you think it was connected to her death?" Lucy pulled a tissue out of her pocket and started to absentmindedly shred it in her lap.

I placed my hands over hers. "Lucy, you're being ridiculous. How could it? I think she ate something she was allergic to and went into anaphylactic shock."

She stared up at me. Fear receded from Lucy's blue eyes. "Really? Do you believe that's what happened?"

I hugged Lucy. "Yes, I do. She was too tough of an old broad to let a silly argument do her in."

A weak smile crossed Lucy's lips. She stood and smoothed out the wrinkles of her wool slacks. "I better get back and help Ralph, the dear man. Hilda's death has me in such a state, he's had to hold down the booth by himself."

I frowned as Lucy hurried over to her husband. She leaned up on tiptoe and planted a kiss on his cheek. Why would Hilda's death have Lucy so upset? Only a few hours ago, she and Hilda had practically come to blows over Hilda selling her pattern designs. Was she remorseful Hilda had died, or was it something more?

I continued on my way to the ladies' room with the dreaded pin clenched in my hand. *Okay, I can do this.* I inhaled a deep breath and pushed open the ladies' room door.

Because the room was still crowded with EMTs and police, no one noticed me. I was surprised to see Doc Cordone, the medical examiner, huddled by the porcelain sinks with Hank and Joe Peters. I thought he would wait to examine Hilda's body when it arrived at the morgue. Wire-rimmed glasses shoved up his head had made his white hair stick straight up. He pointed to his neck and then to Hilda's body now residing on a gurney, zipped into a black bag.

I swallowed hard to keep down the bile that crept up my throat. I wasn't about to embarrass myself and have to rush to the nearest john to empty my breakfast into it.

I didn't want to interrupt the three men, but the pin burned a hole in my hand. I wanted out of here, ASAP.

I cleared my throat. That did the trick and drew their attention to me.

Hank was the first to speak. "Sam, why are you here? This is off-limits now to you ladies."

"Humph," Joe grunted. "As if she ever pays attention to rules."

I chose not to rise to his rude comment. I wanted to hand over the pin and get out of there.

I looked up at Hank with pleading eyes and related how I had found the pin stuck to my sweater and thought it might belong to Hilda.

Joe held out his hand for me to give him the pin. He unwrapped the napkin. "Hank, this matches Doc's and the EMTs' findings."

Hank leaned over and examined the pin. He nodded and said, "You may be right. We'll have to send it in to forensics to have it examined further."

Puzzled by their comments, I asked, "What are you two talking about?"

Joe opened his mouth to say something, but Hank cut him off. Taking my elbow he led me out into the hall. He reached into his pocket and pulled out a small slip of paper. As he opened it up, he asked, "Do you have any idea what this means?"

I shut my eyes and grabbed on to Hank's arm. My legs wobbled so much I feared I'd slip to the floor.

CHAPTER SEVEN

I took a deep breath then read the note Hank held in his rubber-gloved hands.

Hilda,

Please meet me at the end of the hall, down from the ladies' room, ASAP. We must settle our differences. L

I closed my eyes and sent a silent prayer heavenward. *Please, Lord, don't have the signer of this note be who I think it is.*

"Do you have any idea who the 'L' might stand for?" Hank's question snapped me back to earth.

"Umm, I umm. Lots of people have a name beginning with L. Let's see—Linda, Louise, Lois, Layla, Lucky…" I ticked names off my fingers.

"Saaaam," Hank drawled. "Layla, Lucky?"

By the frown creasing his handsome forehead, I figured his patience with me teetered on empty.

Hank tapped a well-polished leather loafer on the tile floor. "I notice you conveniently omitted Lucy."

I bit my bottom lip. "Oh, yeah, Lucy. Did I forget her name? I'm sure she didn't write this note. Customers have swamped her all morning. She couldn't possibly have had time to leave her booth, no matter how angry Hilda made her."

Hank rubbed his forehead.

I clamped a hand over my mouth. "Oops," I said.

The ladies' room door swished open. Doc Cordone poked his head out. "Hank, can you come here a minute?"

"Sure, Doc, in a sec," Hank called over his shoulder. His baby blues never left my face.

Drat. I had stepped in deep doo now. His eyes undid me. They were one reason he was such a great detective. Good thing I'm not a criminal, or I'd blab state secrets if he trained those eyes on me long enough.

"Yeah 'oops,' Sam. What have you kept from me?"

I wrung my fingers and tried to force the words out. "Well, Lucy and Hilda may have engaged in a little tiff earlier this morning. But it amounted to no biggie."

Hank refolded the note and placed it in a plastic bag he pulled out of the back pocket of his tight-fitting jeans.

I swallowed hard. An evidence bag, I presumed.

"What kind of 'tiff' did they have?" he asked.

"Oh, it wasn't anything much. Only a tiny disagreement about some patterns," I said, staring at my shoes. Why did I feel like the little kid caught with her hand in the cookie jar?

Hank reached in his tweed sport jacket and produced a small notebook. "Why don't you let me be the judge of how tiny this disagreement was?"

He pulled a pen from the notebook. "Go on, I'm listening," he said.

Was this the same affectionate man who had cuddled with me on my sofa two nights ago? Where did he go? Who was this cold, stern person standing in front of me?

My spine stiffened. Despite my fond feelings for him, he wouldn't bulldoze me into saying anything I didn't want to. If he thought I'd speak against my good friend Lucy, he could take those cute buns and march them right back into the ladies' room. I'd known her far longer, so there, Detective Hunky Hank. I nodded to myself once for emphasis. Besides, we were standing in the middle of the hall outside the ladies' room. The whole time Hank had questioned me, hookers had passed us on their way to the men's room. I could only imagine the gossip flying around the hook-in now.

"Umm, this morning I overheard Lucy and Hilda discussing a small problem that existed between them."

Hank's pen poised over the notebook. "You aren't going to make this easy, are you, Sam? What kind of problem?"

A smile creased my lips. I could almost feel Hank squirming in his shoes. "They talked about Hilda stealing some of Lucy's rug hooking designs and selling them online as her own."

While Hank jotted this info in his notebook, he asked, "Talked or argued? Do you think Hilda made Lucy mad enough to kill her over the designs?"

I thought back to this morning and Lucy's anger with Hilda. Would she have killed for her designs? I didn't think so, but she had mentioned she hoped she didn't have to take "drastic measures" to stop Hilda from pirating her designs. Would Lucy kill if pushed hard enough by Hilda? After all, the patterns Lucy created from these designs were a big part of her business income. I crossed my fingers behind my back. "No, definitely not. Lucy is a kind, hard-working businesswoman and would never harm anyone. Why would you suspect Lucy, anyway? Hilda's death is a tragic accident, isn't it?"

"I can't say. We're examining all angles of her death. We'll know for sure after the autopsy."

My stomach flipped then flopped. Two cups of coffee and Franny's delicious chocolate chip muffin suddenly hadn't settled too well. An autopsy was such a gruesome procedure. I had attended one once while in college. My boyfriend at the time had majored in criminal justice. He thought viewing an autopsy would be a "neat" date. Observing a person being sliced and diced while the ME devoured a ham sandwich had sent me hoofing it to the nearest ladies' room to deposit my lunch in the toilet. Needless to say, it was my last date with that boyfriend.

The swish of the ladies' room door opening again drew me back to the present.

This time, Joe Peters stuck his balding head out the door. "Detective, we need you in here, now."

"Be right there, Joe," Hank called back, his eyes holding mine. He reached down and squeezed my hand. "Be careful, Sam. You mean a lot to me."

I blinked, and my cheeks burned. Had I heard him right? I meant a lot to him? Sure, we'd been dating for a few months, but he'd never said anything so caring before.

He smiled his crooked smile and turned to reenter the ladies' room.

I needed to splash water on my face to cool down my cheeks. I glanced over at the men's room. Hookers no longer streamed out the door.

I nudged open the door and peeked inside. Can't say I'd ever patronized a men's room before. My eyes traveled around the sterile room. Three urinals hung from the gray-tiled far wall. Two stalls took up space on another. No wonder the line of hookers had snaked down the hallway earlier. Women required a minimum of five stalls to meet their needs. Two sinks graced the third wall. Like the tile, gray was the predominant color theme in the room.

"I saw you talking to the detective. What did he say about Hilda's death?"

I swung around and saw Mari behind me. Her eyes looked bloodshot and her nose red, from crying I guessed.

"Mari, I'm very sorry about your friend's death, but Hank didn't tell me anything about Hilda."

Mari walked over to a sink, pulled a paper towel from the dispenser, and ran it under cold water. She placed the towel over her eyes. After a moment, she removed the towel and threw it in the metal trash can attached to the wall.

She stared at me with a look hard enough to make the blood in my veins run cold. "Hilda told us about her argument with Lucy this morning. I wouldn't put it past Lucy to have done something to cause Hilda's death," she hissed.

My mouth dropped open. "How can you say such a thing, Mari? That isn't true."

"We'll see." Mari turned and marched out of the men's room.

"Lord above. What has Mari's pants in a wad?" Candie asked, breezing into the men's room after Mari left. "I know she's upset by her friend's passing, but she practically steamrolled me down. Close your mouth. You'll catch some flies if you don't."

I did as my cousin instructed and snapped my mouth shut. "How did you find me here?"

"Since you didn't come back to the table and you weren't in the hall scoping out the vendors, I figured this was the only place left to look for you. How did things go with you and Sergeant Peters? You aren't under arrest, are you?"

I shook my head. "Very funny, and no, I'm not under arrest. In fact, I didn't have to deal with him. I talked to Hank."

Candie waggled her ringed fingers at me. "So, tell me, what did he say?"

I related what I had told Hank.

Candie twirled an auburn curl around a slender finger, a sign that she was deep in thought. "Well, hush my mouth. You and I both know Lucy wouldn't hurt a tick."

I nodded in agreement. "You're right. Mari is grieving the loss of her good friend. I'm sure she didn't mean anything."

"Come on, let the Wings Falls Police Department do its job, and join the rest of the Loopy Ladies," Candie said as she scanned the men's room. "Eww. This place is disgusting. It's so dark and gray." She walked over to a chipped sink and stared into the mirror hanging over it. "I certainly couldn't touch up my makeup in this gloom."

I laughed in spite of the dire happenings of the morning. "You do know how to put things in perspective."

My cousin swished by me and winked. "Honey, nothing gets us Southern Belles down."

We talked about the different rugs we saw on hookers' frames as we threaded our way through the crowded room back to our seats. Hilda's death had cast a somber shroud over the hook-in. Usually, the ladies sat chattering away about their latest project or showing off their buys from the vendors. Now heads were bent together whispering about the morning's tragic events. Questioning eyes darted my way. I suppose because I was present at Hilda's death. Fortunately, no one said anything as I passed them.

"Look," Candie said, pointing towards Lucy's booth.

My smile vanished in an instant. Lucy, white as a sheet, clung to Ralph's arm. Joe Peters stood in front of them with arms folded across his ample chest as he questioned her.

CHAPTER EIGHT

"Well, will you take a look-see?" Candie asked.

If I'd been upset at Hank before, consider that a piece of cake. Watching Peters, I feared my blood would boil right out of my veins. Where had his nicey-nicey attitude from earlier today that Lucy spoke about gone?

Even from across the room, I knew Ralph was trying to comfort his wife, but to no avail.

Lucy sat in a folding chair alternately wringing her hands and dabbing at tears running down her cheeks. The only thing Joe Peters missed was shining a naked light bulb in her face.

"I thought he was in the ladies' room. How did he get out here so fast? I need to get Hank." I turned and started back towards the hallway. I had hoped to catch him before he got too involved in the ladies' room.

"Excuse me, excuse me," I mumbled, bumping into chairs on my way to the hall. "Ouch," I said, rubbing my thigh and biting back a curse as a hooker backed her chair into me.

Candie grabbed my arm. "Where do you think you're going?" she asked as I retraced my steps.

I could barely control my anger as I swung around and pointed a shaking finger at Joe. "Hank must stop this interrogation right now. You and I both know Lucy is innocent. But the way he's grilling Lucy, he'll have her confessing to every unsolved mystery on the Wings Falls Police Department books."

"First, take a deep breath and calm down. You know Hank's busy with the coroner," Candie said. "Besides, being all worked up will be about as useful to Lucy as a trap door in a canoe."

My cousin was right. There wasn't much I could do for Lucy right now. Even if I didn't approve of Joe Peters' methods, it was his right to talk to Lucy. Guilt weighed heavily on my shoulders right now since I had told Hank about Lucy and Hilda's falling out earlier this morning.

I heaved a deep sigh and reluctantly agreed. "You're right. Joe would resent me interfering. He'd only take his dislike for me out on Lucy."

Candie chuckled. "Geez, talk about holding a grudge."

I smiled. "Yeah, people about town still call him Sandy." A giggle edged up my throat, and before I knew it, I'd dissolved into full-fledged hysterical laughter. Then sobs shook my body. Candie pulled me to her rather well-endowed chest as tears streamed down my face.

"Oh, Candie, it was horrible. Hilda certainly didn't rank as my BFF, but the way she died…" I blurted out in between hiccupping breaths.

"Here, sit. Let me get you a drink of water." Candie steered me to a metal chair near the kitchen door and ducked inside.

She returned a minute later and placed a plastic cup of cold water in my hands. "Drink," she commanded. "You're only reacting to this horrible morning. First you witnessed the argument between Hilda and Lucy, and then you were present when Hilda died."

My hands trembled. I raised the glass to my mouth and gulped the water as if it were the last ounce on earth. "You're right. It's the stress of the morning. I thought hook-ins were meant to relax a person—you know, mindlessly pulling loops of wool."

"All will work out. The police can handle things, and we'll enjoy the rest of the day. It looks as if they're wrapping up now." Candie nodded towards the end of the hall. EMTs pushed the gurney carrying Hilda's body out of the ladies' room door and towards the rear exit of the banquet hall.

A shiver shot through me. The forceful woman who had arrived at the hook-in this morning now lay zipped into a black plastic bag. Hank and Doc Cordone followed the gurney, heads together, talking as they left. It was evident Hank didn't see me or, at least, give any indication that he did. I frowned at what happened next. A police officer, who'd responded to the initial 9-1-1 call, crisscrossed yellow crime scene tape over the ladies' room door.

"Look." I pointed at the officer. "What do you think that means?"

Candie's violet eyes followed my finger. "It certainly is strange if this is an ordinary death. The police must believe something more is involved."

I frowned. "Like what?" I asked. "Hilda went into anaphylactic shock from something she ate." Her death was cut and dry to me, but then, I did find a goodie bag pin with blood on it stuck to my sweater. Hank acted very interested when I brought it to his attention.

"What's going on beneath those curls of yours?" my cousin asked.

Unconsciously, I ran my fingers through my mop of brown curls, the bane of my existence. These curls, which I inherited from my Memaw Parker, knew a life of their own. I tried to tame them with a comb, gels, and lotions, but they insisted on springing whichever way they desired.

After relaying my thoughts to her, I asked, "So, do you think there's more to Hilda's death?"

"Let me call Mark and ask if he knows anything." Candie pulled out her cell phone and pushed what I assumed was Mark's speed dial button on her phone. I figured it was there because he was her current boyfriend. Since he was the mayor of Wings Falls, I was certain that the police would have informed him of any suspicious death occurring in his town.

Candie asked Mark what he knew of Hilda's death, and after several *umm*s and *ah-hah*s, she ended the call, but not without sending him a few air smooches.

Impatient for the answer, I waggled my fingers at her and said, "So what did he say?"

She slipped the phone back into her pocket. "Hank's been in touch with Mark, and he's not ruling out homicide."

"Homicide?" I squeaked.

Candie nodded and placed a slender finger to her mouth. "Shh. They discovered a mark on her neck, and coupled with the pin you gave Hank, it was suspicious to them. Now, this is all on the QT, so mum's the word to anyone."

The blood drained from my face. Another murder in Wings Falls and me discovering it or at least present when the victim died. Why me? Was I a murder magnet? No, it couldn't be happening again.

"Sam, are you all right? You look like you saw a ghost." My cousin took the shaking glass of water from my hand. She must have feared I'd spill it all over myself.

The kitchen door swung open. Franny stepped into the hallway, wiping her brown hands on an apron. Scents of something heavenly baking wafted out into the hall behind her. She was not a classically trained chef, and by that, I mean she wasn't a culinary school graduate, but she had learned from the best—her Southern memaw. No one, and I mean no one, baked a better pecan pie than Franny. When she featured her bread pudding with bourbon sauce on her restaurant's menu, a line wound outside Sweetie Pie's door.

"What a morning," Franny said. "That poor Miss Pratt. Sam, you all right? You are a might pale."

"I'm fine. I think this morning's events have rattled me." What an understatement.

"Wait here. Let me fetch one of my sweet potato muffins. It will perk you up." Franny turned and retreated into the kitchen. More delicious aromas of food being prepared for lunch escaped from the kitchen.

A rumble sounded from Candie. "Candie, is your stomach calling out for a taste of Franny's Southern cooking?" I couldn't blame her. Franny's delicious cuisine would make the most diet-conscious person drool.

"I do miss my breaded, fried porkchops and turnip greens." Candie rolled her eyes towards the ceiling and licked her lips. "Oh, to dive into a piece of Memaw's banana cream pie right now…" Her chest rose and fell in a deep sigh, fluttering the ruffles on her blouse.

The kitchen door opened, framing Franny. She carried two plates, each laden with a muffin.

Franny held the plates out to us. "Here you go, Sam, and one for you, too, Candie."

Candie reached for the muffin. "One for me, too? You are an angel."

"Why of course. You don't think I'd forget you, since we are practically kin, both coming from the South? And I know what a good cook you are, too."

I coughed and choked on the muffin crumbs. One thing my cousin and I could not do was cook. Our Memaw Parker lamented over Candie's and my lack of cooking skills. She considered it the one great failure in her life. Candie had never showed any interest, as she was too busy flirting with the boys. Me, I was too busy writing down the stories that crowded my brain. Pushing the buttons on a microwave strained the extent of our kitchen skills.

An idea struck me. "Franny, I know you've been busy in the kitchen all morning, but did you happen to notice anything strange going on out here in the hallway?"

"Let me think on it a minute. As you can imagine, I was busy, but I did leave the kitchen a time or two." With a long, slender brown finger, Franny tapped the side of her forehead as she thought. "Oh, yes, I remember. The kitchen was steaming up pretty good, what with muffins baking in the oven and getting the chicken pot pie ready for lunch. It's a good thing this banquet hall has more than one stove. Don't know how'd I do it, feeding all you hungry women. Nothing worse than a room full of starving hookers. Yep, right after I'd pulled a batch of those sweet potato muffins you're enjoying out of the oven. I'd set them on the counter to cool for a few minutes and decided I needed a breather before tackling the pot pies and stepped into the hall. Loud voices were coming from down there. Shouting, to be exact." Franny nodded towards the far end of the hallway.

"Loud voices? Shouting?" I asked around a mouthful of muffin. "Who was arguing?"

"That large lady, Miss Pratt. She acted real riled up about something. And another lady, I'm not sure who she is. She's only come into the restaurant a couple of times. But she sure had her tail feathers twisted in a knot. Pointing a finger and getting right into Miss Pratt's face. I think if I hadn't gasped and they hadn't noticed me, she would have hauled off and landed a right good punch on Miss Pratt's nose."

"Can you describe her? Short, tall, skinny, fat?" my cousin asked, flicking crumbs off the front of her blouse.

I wanted to give her a high-five for asking what my overwrought brain refused to compute.

Franny wrinkled her forehead in thought. "Hmm, let me think. She wasn't skinny, but she wasn't fat, either."

My brain finally unfroze as I asked a few intelligent questions. "Color hair? Can you remember what she wore?"

"Hair color? Blonde. I think it was blonde." Franny nodded. "Yes, I'm positive, blonde, but if you ask me, it's right out of a bottle." Franny chuckled.

"Straight, curly?" I asked, a picture of the woman Hilda argued with forming in my mind's eye.

"Curly, definitely curly, but not as curly as mine." Franny smiled. She ran a hand through her tight black curls.

"One last question. Did she wear large, red-framed glasses?" I asked. I was almost certain that I knew the identity of this woman.

"Why, yes, she did. Do you know her?" Franny asked.

Candie and I looked at each other and nodded. "Roberta Holden," we both said at the same time.

CHAPTER NINE

———

"Roberta Holden," I mumbled to myself again.

Candie nodded. "Now what could Roberta and Hilda have been arguing about? Roberta did mention losing money in a bad investment. Do you think it amounted to more than she said?"

I stood—the folding chair had started to numb my buns—and thanked Franny for the delicious muffin. Fellow hookers passed by us and complemented Franny on the morning's breakfast fare.

Franny extracted herself from her culinary admirers and said, "Lunch and the kitchen are shouting to me. I hope the muffins picked you ladies up a bit."

"They did wonders. Thank you so much. We're looking forward to lunch." I crumpled the paper plate that held my muffin and scanned the hallway for a trash can.

"Sweetie, here, let me have your plate. As I said, I need to get back to preparing lunch. Can't have a pack of hungry hookers on my hands. Who knows what they'd do? I don't think that would be a pretty sight. Oh, dear, I guess I was a little insensitive, what with Miss Pratt passing." Pink tinged Franny's dark cheeks.

I grabbed Franny's hand. In spite of her hard work in the kitchen, it was soft and smooth. "Don't give it another thought. There's not a mean bone in your body. You're only stating the obvious. Even a person's passing wouldn't stop a hungry group of hookers from mobbing the buffet table."

Candie patted Franny's back. "Sam's right. Don't dare get between a hooker and your fabulous food. There could be dire consequences."

A weak smile spread across her face. "Thank you, ladies. I'd better get back to work." Franny turned and pushed open the kitchen door. The sounds of pots clanking, oven doors shutting, water running, and the voices of her helpers busy preparing lunch for the hookers escaped from the kitchen.

Alone in the hall, after Franny returned to her kitchen duties, I turned to Candie and asked the question burning the tip of my tongue. "Do you think Roberta killed Hilda?"

My cousin shrugged. "I don't know. Anyone, if they were pushed hard enough, could kill someone. But what would be Roberta's motive? Sure, she might not like it if Hilda caused her and her husband to lose some money, but she implied it wasn't very much."

"But what if she lied? If I remember correctly, Roberta loved being a stay-at-home mom, but suddenly she took a job at the Only A Dollar discount store. Her Billy was five years old then. She always talked about how much she enjoyed raising him. It surprised me when I saw her behind the register there. I had run in to get a birthday card for Memaw. I asked about her new job, but she became flustered and said she needed some out-of-the-house time. She said she craved adult conversation once in a while."

Deep in thought, Candie tapped the side of her head with her fingernail. "Hmm," she said. "I don't know the particulars of her working, but maybe she told us a fib about not losing a bunch of money. What if she and Clyde lost a lot more money than she said and she needed to go to work?"

"But, Candie, it happened years ago. Why wait until now to do her in?"

Candie nodded in agreement. Wisps of auburn hair floated about her face. "Yes, but you know Hilda—tactful wasn't her middle name. Maybe she needled Roberta about losing the money, and Roberta finally snapped. Hilda could have tried the patience of a saint."

"That's the understatement of the year. Anyway, there's nothing to say that she didn't die of natural causes." I glanced down the hall to the ladies' room and spied the yellow crime scene tape crisscrossed over the door. I thought about the soundness of Candie's theory.

Voices pulled me out of my depressing thoughts. A group of hookers, heading towards the men's room, interrupted our alone time in the hallway. When they saw me, their conversation came to an abrupt halt. A hooker in pink sweatpants and matching sweatshirt (shoot me if I ever start wearing my sweats in public as a fashion statement) pointed to me and said to her companions, "*She* was there when dear Hilda died. Didn't she find a dead body last year, too?"

"Mighty peculiar, if you ask me," another replied, this one dressed in a jogging suit. I considered this an upgrade from the sweatsuit, but not by much.

Heads bobbed in agreement to her answer.

What? Did I have a big "M" for murderer stitched to the front of my wool sweater? Because it's my misfortune to be at the demise of two people doesn't make me responsible. Unlucky, yes, but the cause, no.

I stepped forward to defend myself against their verbal attack, but Candie grabbed my elbow.

"Old biddies will gossip. There's no way you can stop these magpies from chattering," Candie said, loud enough for the retreating ladies to hear.

"But," I stammered, lucky to get out one word. My body shook with rage at the group's unfeeling comments.

"We all know, including the police, that you are not involved with these deaths." My cousin did her best to calm me down.

Taking a deep breath, I nodded. "You're right. Let's go back to our table and get some hooking done. After all, it's what we're here for."

A smile spread across Candie's face, and freckles danced across her nose. "Yep, but don't forget eating and buying more wool."

I wanted to laugh but I quickly stifled it. The morning's events didn't mesh with laughter. I slid my arm through Candie's and steered her towards our table. I said, "You've got the true mission of a hooker down: pull loops, eat, and buy more wool."

As we wove our way across the room, I felt eyes boring into my back. Some ladies pointed at me. Others grew silent as we passed their table. Until the medical examiner issued his report on the cause of Hilda's death, I guess this constituted my new norm of treatment. Would people avoid me because they thought I was a harbinger of death? I lifted my chin a notch higher. So be it. True friends stick by you.

As if to prove my point, smiles and questions for my concern greeted me when I arrived at the Loopy Ladies' table.

I settled in my chair and returned my friends' smiles with a weak one of my own.

"So, what did Junior say about Hilda's death?" Gladys asked, looking up from her hooking.

I smiled. Gladys was Hank's aunt, and much to his chagrin, at forty-five, she still called him by his childhood nickname.

I scanned the table and saw that all hooking had stopped. Since I dated the investigating detective, I guess I was the inside source for all things Hilda-related. "He didn't have much to say other than to question me about the events surrounding Hilda's death."

Not one to miss an opportunity for gossip, Helen Garber leaned her ample body over her hooking frame and asked, "On my way to the bathroom, I noticed yellow crime scene tape tacked to the ladies' room door." She paused to screw her face up in disgust. "Why would they put tape on the door if she died naturally? That's mighty suspicious if you ask me."

Heads bobbed in agreement to her statement.

"What about the pin stuck to your sweater? Does it have anything to do with Hilda's death?" Cookie Harrington asked. She was the newest member of the Loopy Ladies, but she was fast becoming an accomplished hooker. Stretched across her frame was a pattern featuring a cat playing with a ball of yarn. It looked like her job as receptionist at the Wings Falls Animal Hospital was influencing her hooking.

My stomach clenched. I couldn't reveal all the interest Hank, Joe, and especially the medical examiner had paid to the pin when I showed it to them. Hank trusted me not to share what I had learned while in the ladies' room. But what did I know, other than Hilda's pin had blood on it, presumably her blood?

"Ladies, Hank is a professional. I may be dating him, but he isn't going to share with me the particulars of any case he's involved with." I pushed my bangs out of my eyes and hoped my answer put a stop to any more questions.

"Pssh, pillow talk," Gladys said in a tone barely above a whisper. Fingers gnarled with arthritis, she picked up her hook.

My eyes widened at her remark. "What?" I asked.

"I've noticed his car leaving your house in the early morning hours. Don't tell me the two of you sit there and watch late-night talk shows until the sun is practically up."

Candie giggled and then became so engrossed in her rug pattern of baby ducks and their mother one would think she pulled loops of golden floss.

Heat crawled up my neck. I never thought of Gladys keeping track of my love life, since it was nonexistent before Hank. Before him, my only late-night activity consisted of Porkchop's pre-bedtime walk.

Patsy Ikeda pointed her hook towards the front of the banquet hall. "I wonder what that's all about."

I swiveled in my seat and saw Joe Peters, flanked by three uniformed policemen, walking towards the front. He halted by a table set up near the door that Lucy had used as a check-in point when hookers first arrived this morning. I cringed as I thought of all the excitement that had transpired since we had arrived this morning. Was it only a few hours ago that we were all happily checking in, finding our tables, and spreading out our rug hooking gear?

Joe cleared his throat to get the attention of the room full of chattering ladies. When this failed, he shouted above the din, "Ladies, may I have quiet, please?"

Marybeth Higgins laughed. "Good luck." Quieting a room full of hookers was not going to be an easy task.

"This is official Wings Falls Police business, and I want quiet!" shouted Joe. The officers at his side winced at his attention-getting loud voice.

I shook my head. "That's Smooth Joe for you. He always knows how to win people over. What's so important he has other officers for backup? Hilda has already left the building."

"We're about to find out," Candie said as hookers started to obey his order and quieted down.

Soon, only the sounds of plates clattering and silverware clinking, emanating from the kitchen, filtered into the room.

Joe motioned to the three policemen standing next to him. "We will call you up to this table one at a time to take the names and contact information of everyone in this banquet hall." Joe turned and pointed to Lucy's sign-in table. "So please stay seated until they are finished. No one, and I mean no one, is to leave this room until I say so."

"But what if I have to go to the bathroom?" an unhappy hooker in the rear of the hall shouted out.

"Franny will serve lunch soon. You don't expect us to miss lunch, do you?" added another equally distressed voice.

"Sounds like Joe has his hands full. The natives are getting restless. Never stand between a hooker and a buffet line," Gladys said, looking up from her hooking.

"I have to agree." I turned back to my table and noticed Roberta Holden's still-empty chair. Where was she? I glanced down the hall where Franny had last seen her. I stared at the ever-present yellow tape draping the ladies' room door. *Isn't this a bit much even for Joe if Hilda's death is an accident?*

CHAPTER TEN

My thoughts must have conjured her up because I spied Roberta walking down the hallway leading from the restrooms. I elbowed Candie in the ribs, which elicited a frown from her. I nodded in Roberta's direction.

Candie's Passion Pink lips formed into an O. "The prodigal hooker returns."

"You could say so. Where do you think she's been?" By the snow that nested on her hair and was quickly melting on the shoulders of her sweater, I gathered outside.

"I'm sure your curious mind will find out. No one can stand your grilling questions. You might as well get out the rubber hose."

My cousin leaned sideways to miss another of my jabs to the ribs for her sassy remark.

With a welcoming smile on my face, I greeted Roberta as she reclaimed her seat at our table. "Are you okay? We were worried about you, what with all the excitement this morning. You're kind of pale."

Candie whipped her head around and glared at me. Okay, so I poured it on a little thick, but if this got me some answers, so be it.

Roberta raked a hand through her hair, dislodging the few remaining snowflakes. She settled her hooking frame in front of her and said, "I snuck out to my car for a smoke." With a shrug and a half laugh, she continued, "I know, I know. I need to quit."

Helen Garber, who sat next to the delinquent member of the group, waved a hand in front of her nose and scooted her chair a few inches away from Roberta. "Whew, I can vouch for her smoking. She smells like a blocked-up chimney." Tact had never been Helen's middle name.

Roberta's lips trembled. "Sorry. Would you like me to move?"

I jumped in and tried to prevent Roberta from having a complete breakdown. "We all know how hard you've tried to stop smoking, but like any bad habit, we have all fallen off that old wagon at times. Let's enjoy what's left of the afternoon and get some serious hooking done."

Helen harrumphed at my attempt to smooth things over. Roberta flashed me a tremulous smile.

What could have sent Roberta over the edge to start smoking again after declaring only last week she had "kicked the habit"? And what made her so jittery?

I shook my head, determined not to read anything more into this morning's events. One by one the officers called ladies to the table at the front of the hall to ask questions and record any information they saw necessary. Even with all these interruptions, the Loopy Ladies settled into an afternoon of hooking, gabbing, and eating.

"How is your book coming?" Marybeth Higgins asked.

I smiled and laid my hook down. My children's book, *Porkchop, the Wonder Dog,* held a place next to my heart.

"Really well. My editor, Bob Spellman, called the other day and set next January as the publishing date. We have so much to do before then. Porkchop will be one busy dog. Which means I'll be busy, too."

Jane Burrows looked up from her rug. "Not too busy for a reading at the library, I hope?"

"I've placed the library first on my list for book readings. You corral the kids, and Porkchop and I will be there." I picked up my hook and pulled more loops. I wanted to finish this rug. My fingers itched to start my Porkchop rug. After that rug, a pattern in Lucy's booth for my dining room table had caught my eye. It featured a row of primitive pumpkins of various shapes and sizes. The center pumpkin overflowed with American flags. The color plan in my head called for orange, white, and green pumpkins. Like most of us who loved to pull strips of wool, the next rug always begged for attention before the current one came off the frame.

"What does your editor want you and Porkchop to do before publication?" Patsy Ikeda asked.

I smiled, encouraged that she had actually asked me a question, since I wasn't her favorite person because I had suspected her of murdering the owner of a local animal shelter last fall.

"Bob wants to publish a calendar featuring Porkchop," I said, grinning to myself at the possible outfits he'd wear for each month. Would he be Cupid for February? Maybe for November he would don a pilgrim's hat? Or what about a yellow raincoat and hat for April's showers? Ideas ran rampant through my brain.

"And to think I live next door to a star." Gladys clasped her hands and rolled her eyes towards the stained drop ceiling. "I can say 'I knew him when.'"

Laughter erupted around the table at Gladys's proclamation.

Throughout the afternoon of hooking and gabbing, I kept an eye on Roberta. While she had joined in the conversations that sprang up around the table, was it my imagination, or was she unusually nervous? I swear her hook shook as she worked on her rug. What upset her so? The real giveaway came when the police had wanted to interview our table. Most of the ladies saw it as an adventure, something out of the ordinary from their everyday lives. Gladys couldn't wait to tell her Pookie Bear and live-in boyfriend, Frank Gilbert, about the day's events. I say most of the ladies, because when it came to Roberta's turn, all the color drained from her face and sweat beaded her forehead. If we weren't squeezed around the table so tightly, she'd have fallen off her chair and landed in a heap on the hall's cold tile floor.

"What do you make of Roberta?" I whispered out of the side of my mouth to Candie.

"What? What?" Candie blinked and looked around the room.

I rolled my eyes and said, "Oh, please, didn't you notice how Roberta reacted when she was called to the front of the room?"

My cousin shook her head. "Can't say that I did. I'm not pleased with this duck." She pointed to her pattern. She'd hooked the momma duck and was now working on one of the three baby ducks. I shrugged since her hooking had looked fine to me.

Had I made more out of Roberta's reaction than necessary? I mean, talking to the police frightens some people even in the most normal of circumstances, and today certainly didn't qualify as normal.

My cousin now gave me her full attention. "How did she look?"

"I think she'd be in a better mood if the IRS put a lien on all of her belongings."

"There's Hank. I think he wants you," Candie said, pointing with her hook towards the hallway.

I glanced towards the hallway and saw Hank motion with his hand for me to join him. I pushed aside wool, coffee mugs, and paper plates filled with partially eaten goodies left from the lunch buffet and laid my hooking equipment on the table. Neatness goes by the wayside when hookers concentrate on their craft.

I snaked through tables of ladies bent over hooking frames and indulging in whatever ranked as the latest gossip amongst their group as I made my way to Hank. My heart squeezed in my chest the closer I got to him. His Fred Flintstone tie (he had a weakness for cartoon-inspired ties) hung loosened at his neck. His brown hair was disheveled, I was sure from raking his fingers through it as he dealt with the circumstances of Hilda's death. And, I imagined, contending with Joe Peters, who could be a wee bit full of himself, would be trying. Joe did tend to walk around puffed up with his own self-importance, perhaps left over from his high school days on the football team. Of course, he leaves out the fact that he had warmed the bench more than he had played.

As I drew nearer to Hank, a smile spread across his face, erasing some of the tiredness clouding it a few moments before. I matched his smile. Darn, if I couldn't help myself. My fingers reached up and smoothed back the brown curl with a mind of its own that constantly slipped down onto his forehead. His vibrant blue eyes stared into mine. He pulled me farther into the hallway, away from the crowded main room and the staring eyes of its occupants. He leaned down and kissed me gently on my lips. Snow wasn't the only thing melting today. I would have ended in a puddle on the floor if he'd continued.

"You've come back. How are things going?" I asked, trying to settle my racing heart and bring myself back to earth.

Hank straightened and ran his fingers through his hair, which caused the errant curl to lodge on his forehead again. "I just needed another glimpse of you. But to answer your question, as well as can be expected with Peters here."

I smoothed my fingers over Fred Flintstone then gazed up at Hank with hopeful eyes. "Any chance of us having dinner together tonight?"

He shook his head. "I'm afraid I'll have to pass. I want to wait at the station for Hilda's blood results."

"You can get them that fast?" I asked.

"You'd be surprised what technology can do today," he said, gently pushing a stray strand of hair behind my ear.

I looked up and smiled. "Well, when you're done, you can always stop by my house for a beer. And you know your favorite admirer would love a scratch behind the ears."

Hank's eyes crinkled as he laughed. "You want me to scratch you behind the ears?"

I swatted at his jacket. "No, silly. Porkchop. He misses you."

"He's the only one who misses me and needs some care?" Hank teased back.

Heat crawled up my neck as I thought of the kind of attention I'd love from Hank. "I wouldn't mind some consideration, too."

His strong, calloused hand cradled my neck. "If it's not too late, I'll try to stop by."

"Promise?" I asked, hope filling my voice.

"Promise," he whispered against my ear. "I've got to get back to work."

My eyes followed him as he turned and walked down the hall.

Back at my table, I picked up my hook and spent the rest of the afternoon hooking, browsing the vendors, eating, and pondering what had caused Hilda's death.

"Ready to go, cuz?"

I glanced up at Candie with a quizzical expression then down at my watch. The hands pointed to five o'clock. "Geez, the day has flown." My eyes scanned the banquet hall, and sure enough, hookers were packing up their rugs and equipment.

"The day's events and my hooking must have absorbed my attention. I didn't even notice people leaving."

Candie shoved her equipment into her woven basket. "It certainly was an interesting hook-in. Will you see Hank tonight?"

I grabbed my red canvas bag off the floor and shoved my rug and frame into it. "He said he probably would be too busy to stop by, but Porkchop and I will cross our fingers and paws in hopes that he can."

Candie laughed. We grabbed our bags and the purchases we hadn't been able to resist and waved goodbye to our fellow Loopy Ladies.

* * *

I tugged the red and white afghan Memaw Parker had crocheted for my eighteenth birthday up to my chin. Something weighed it down. I lifted my head and discovered the cause of my problem—Porkchop. We both fought for space and the blanket on my chintz-covered sofa. I hesitated to go to bed. I still hoped Hank might show up tonight. I craned my neck to read the time on the schoolhouse clock that hung above my television on the wall next to my fireplace. Nine o'clock.

"We can turn the lights out and head to bed, Porkchop. Maybe we'll both get a decent night's sleep."

My dog cocked his head and stared at me with his HERSHEY-brown eyes. His head swiveled towards the door. He jumped off the sofa and dragged the afghan with him.

"Thanks, buddy," I called after him. The sudden loss of my covering left me chilled.

A knock sounded on the door, followed by a voice calling my name. Hank! It was Hank. He'd made it after all.

I sprang off the sofa and ran to the door, tripping on the blanket Porkchop dragged behind him. A quick glance in the mirror hanging by the door revealed a head full of curls standing on end. I wet my fingers and tried, in vain, to tame them into place.

"Sam, are you all right?" Hank called through the door.

I twisted the lock and yanked open the door to a very weary detective. His sport coat looped through a finger, draped over his shoulder. Fred Flintstone was stuffed into a shirt pocket.

"I'm fine, but you look a little tired." I grabbed his free hand and led him to the sofa.

He leaned his head back against a cushion and sighed. "It's been a long and interesting day."

I stared down at this man who made my heart skip a beat. "Can I get you something to eat or drink? Coffee, a beer?"

"A beer would be great," he said as his eyes drooped shut.

I retreated to my kitchen. It saw its last renovation in the 80s when my parents had owned the house. They signed it over to me right before they moved to sunny Florida five years ago. The Coppertone appliances were still functioning. The worn vinyl flooring and chipped Formica countertops served their purpose. The cabinets weren't too bad. They were made of solid wood. Maybe if Porkchop's book became a success, I could afford a kitchen redo. Maybe. Rummaging around in the fridge, I grabbed a Trail's Head IPA. Hank's favorite. I skipped a glass, as he preferred his beer straight from the bottle.

When I returned to the living room, soft snores came from the sofa. I smiled, pulled Memaw's blanket over him, and turned off the light on the end table next to the sofa.

I backtracked to the kitchen. The refrigerator door's hinges groaned. I placed the beer back onto a shelf. Luckily, I hadn't removed the cap. It could wait for another day.

I'd sleep on my dad's old recliner across from the sofa. It might be worn, and the corduroy was frayed on the arms. Stains dotted the cushion, but it remained a big reminder of him. My memory was filled with the two of us cradled in the overstuffed chair while he read my favorite story, *Charlotte's Web,* for the thousandth time. But back in the living room, I noticed the blanket had slipped off Hank onto the floor. As I picked it up and tucked it around his shoulders, he mumbled one word.

"Arsenic."

CHAPTER ELEVEN

"Arsenic?" I whispered into the night-shadowed room. Porkchop, the traitor, nestled his sausage-shaped body against Hank on the sofa, lifting his head. "Yes, Porkie, he said arsenic."

I gasped. "Do you think the medical examiner's report showed they found some in Hilda's blood stream? If so, it would mean..." The reality of the one-word Hank murmured in his sleep hit me—someone murdered Hilda. The chatter floating around the hook-in had alluded to it, but now to have it confirmed, even if by a sleeping man... A shiver shot through my body.

Someone, a hooker possibly, in that cavernous banquet hall had committed murder. I shook my head and tried to erase that thought. It wasn't possible—not the ladies I knew. They were all so sweet. Well, most of them anyway. Every group has an oddball or two. The aches and pains of middle age affected most of us too much to contemplate murder. No, Hank's dream must have been of another case, not Hilda's. "Right, Porkchop?"

My dog cocked his head at me then closed his eyes. In a few seconds, his soft snores joined Hank's.

Well, so much for my dog's interest in my musings. Weary from the day's events, my eyes drifted closed, too.

*   *   *

"Open your mouth. Take this medicine. Good girl. A little wider. Come on, my pretty. I said open your mouth. Now!"
I shook my head and tried to dodge the giant spoon that loomed over me. I wouldn't let the witch win. I didn't care how many yards of wool she promised me. No way would I swallow the foul-smelling concoction she tried to force on me.

"Sam, Sam. Wake up!"

I peeled open my eyelids. Hank stood over me, gently shaking my shoulder.

I pushed the recliner into a sitting position and blinked. Porkchop jumped onto my lap. I stroked his fur to calm my trembling hands. "What happened?"

"You shouted in your sleep 'Stop! Stop!' You must have been having a nightmare."

"Yeah, I guess you could say a nightmare grabbed hold of my sweet dreams." I rubbed my eyes, trying to erase it away.

Hank's eyes were filled with concern. "Want to talk about it?"

I hesitated and glanced down at my hands as I rubbed Porkchop's sleek back. "I think something you said triggered my nightmare."

Hank raised an eyebrow at my statement. "What did I say?"

"While you were asleep, you mumbled the word arsenic. Tell me it has nothing to do with Hilda's death, puh-leese." I drawled out the last word and crossed my fingers (and eyes and toes), hoping against hope. I prayed the good Lord would protect us from anything connected to murder.

Hank lowered his eyes to Porkchop and added his strong hand to mine, stroking my dog's soft fur.

"Someone murdered Hilda, didn't they?" I whispered. The room was eerily silent except for the schoolhouse clock. It sounded like Big Ben as it ticked away the night's minutes.

Hank raised his head. His crystal-blue eyes searched mine. He grasped my hand, nodding slightly. "Yes, I'm afraid we suspect that she was murdered. At least that is the medical examiner's findings."

I swallowed and asked, "With arsenic?"

Again, he gave a slight nod.

"How could it have happened? We all ate the same food. Her friends surrounded her the whole time she was in the banquet hall. She loved being the center of attention."

"Remember the hook-shaped pin stuck to your sweater? The one you returned to us?"

"Yes, but my fingerprints smudged any other prints by the time I gave it to you." Geez, what was I doing? Confessing to Hilda's murder? Hank and I might be dating, but I'm sure if he thought I had killed her, he'd usher me into his car right now, and not for a ride to the local Dairy Queen for my favorite dish of soft-serve chocolate ice cream smothered in chocolate sprinkles, either. Nope, more like a quick trip to the Wings Falls Police Station, where Joe Peters would do a happy dance and take great pleasure as he processed me for the murder of Hilda Pratt.

Hank grinned. "At least you weren't chewing on the evidence like Porkchop did when you found Calvin Perkins' body."

I cringed, thinking of last August when I had stumbled upon the body of the owner of the local pet shelter. Once again, only trying to do a good deed, I wanted to donate a bag of dog food Porkchop had turned his nose up at in disgust. I thought the dogs at the shelter might welcome the treat. Instead, I became embroiled in his murder investigation. But I did have to give myself a pat on the back since I had solved the crime.

I jerked my thoughts back to the present and asked, "What does the pin have to do with her death? I mean, it's such a tiny thing. We're not talking a gun or a knife."

Hank shook his head. That wayward brown curl of his fell onto his forehead. This time I couldn't help myself and reached up and brushed it back. His sweet smile, my reward. "You know allergies plagued her."

I nodded and said, "That was why she carried an Epi Pen. Well, obviously not all the time since she didn't have it with her in the ladies' room."

"It looks like arsenic, even the smallest amount, was highly lethal to her. The lab tested the pin, and traces of the poison covered it."

I gasped. "So, someone deliberately killed her. How did they administer the poison?"

"When the EMTs examined her body, they noted a small spot of blood on her neck. They pointed it out to me, and I, in turn, showed the medical examiner, Doc Cordone. We figure whoever killed her jabbed the pin into her neck."

I shivered. Who had hated Hilda so much to kill her in such a horrible way? And they must have known Hilda would die an agonizing death. They probably figured she'd die alone, too. They didn't count on me having a call of nature and finding her. Were they seeking revenge for something Hilda did to them? If so, who? Blinking, I answered my own question. I thought of a few in the Loopy Ladies I wouldn't call Hilda's BFFs: Jane Burrows, Roberta Holden, Lucy Foster. No way, nope, never—my friends couldn't possibly have killed her. But then a niggle of doubt inched into my brain. Even the nicest person could do something bad given the right push. Someone else Hilda had angered must have attended the hook-in and wanted her dead. After all, there were a hundred people there. But who?

Hank stood and placed his hands on his hips. He frowned and said, "I see that expression on your face. You're not thinking of getting involved in this investigation, are you?"

I feigned an innocent look. "What look?"

"You know, your brow wrinkled, deep in thought."

I laughed. "Because I'm absorbing what you said doesn't mean I'm going to go all Nancy Drew." I wish I'd said this with a little more conviction. I wouldn't abandon any of my friends if they needed my help.

He reached out for my hand and pulled me into his arms. Porkchop jumped at our feet.

"Good," he said, nuzzling my neck. "You mean too much to me. I don't want anything to happen to you."

I answered by taking his hand and leading him down the hall to my bedroom. Porkchop trotted over to his bed by the fireplace, content to curl up and fall asleep.

* * *

Candie leaned back against the red vinyl booth. "Is my company so boring?"

We sat in our usual spot to enjoy Sunday morning breakfast at Sweetie Pie's Café. We came here after the 10:00 a.m. Mass at Saint Anthony's. Our booth looked out on Main Street. Franny Goodway, the same Franny who had catered the hook-in yesterday, had moved north over fifteen years ago and opened her restaurant. She'd decorated the cafe with a welcoming and fun '50s décor. Nothing fancy. Booths of red vinyl hugged three of the glossy white walls. A checkerboard pattern of black and white tile covered the floor. Red vinyl also covered the stools tucked under the counter on the kitchen wall. As usual, a group of local senior gentlemen occupied them. They solved the world's problems while downing cups of Franny's hot and delicious coffee. Her menu offered the best Southern-style cooking north of the Mason Dixon Line.

I stifled a yawn and picked up the menu a waitress had delivered to our table a few minutes earlier. "Of course not. Why do you ask?"

"See what I mean? You're about to fall asleep right there in your seat. It was all you could do to keep your eyes open during Father Pete's sermon." My cousin tapped her ruby-red-painted fingernails on the scratched red Formica tabletop. Red ruled the color scheme in Sweetie Pie's.

I ignored her question and flipped through the song selection of the jukebox at the end of our table. If I gave the box a good smack, like the Fonz in *Happy Days*, would a song belt out?

"You're not paying attention to me," Candie drawled out in her best Southern accent.

"If you must know, I didn't sleep much last night." I knew I should confess now, or she'd never let up.

Candie pointed a ringed finger at me. "Hilda's death isn't still bothering you, is it? You aren't to blame no matter what anyone says."

I leaned over the table and whispered so no one else in the restaurant could hear. "Well, of course I know I'm not to blame." I straightened up. My spine went rigid as her statement hit me. "Wait a minute. Who says I *am* to blame for her death?"

Candie's flushed face almost matched her auburn hair. "No one important, but I set them straight. Anyway, you don't mess with us Parkers." Candie nodded for emphasis.

"Who? I want names." It was best to know who you're up against right from the start.

Candie stared down at the table. "Mari Adams."

"And? Who else?" I persisted.

"Only Mari. Remember, I needed to go to the restroom before we left the hook-in?"

I nodded. I had wanted to avoid the restroom until I got home.

"She was in there, too. She mouthed off to some of her group. But don't worry. I told her a thing or two—you know, about how you tried to save Hilda's life."

I covered her hand with mine and gave it a squeeze. "You are a treasure, dear cousin. Thank you for sticking up for me. I know I didn't have anything to do with her death, but someone did."

Candie's violet eyes widened. "You mean someone murdered her?"

I placed my finger to my lips. "Shhh!" I leaned in closer and whispered, "They suspect someone poisoned her."

"How do you know?"

Now it was my turn to blush. "Hank stopped by late last night. He talked in his sleep and accidentally mentioned the word arsenic."

Candie's eyes widened in surprise. "Arsenic?"

She sat silently and twisted a paper napkin in her fingers as I related what Hank had told me the night before about what the medical examiner's report had revealed.

"Murder," Candie breathed out. "Did Hank mention any possible suspects?"

I shook my head. "Not yet, but knowing him, he's on top of everything."

A smile spread across my cousin's face. "So is Hank the reason you're so tired this morning? Did he spend the night?"

I didn't have to answer. The heat I felt crawling up my neck said it all.

Candie rubbed her hands together. "Good for you, Sam. Now we have to get to work and prove you didn't poison Hilda."

My jaw dropped almost to the tabletop. "What are you talking about? You know I'm innocent."

"You and I know it, but what about Sergeant Peters and Hilda's friends, especially Mari Adams? Their fingers will all point to you since she died with you present."

"Ladies, you ready to order, yet?"

I turned to our waitress, a new girl dressed in Sweetie Pie's standard pink uniform with a black and white checked collar. She wore a matching apron cinched around her small waist. A lace-trimmed handkerchief flowed out of a breast pocket. I opened my mouth, but nothing came out. Suddenly, I couldn't face my usual Sunday bowl of grits with an order of bacon on the side. Not with the thought of having to prove my innocence—again.

CHAPTER TWELVE

———

"I'm stuffed." Candie flopped against the back of the booth. She rubbed her stomach and groaned. Her breakfast plate sat naked of the pancakes topped with strawberries and a mound of whipped cream the waitress had laid before her only twenty minutes before. She leaned closer to me and in a hushed voice whispered, "Franny's flapjacks could give Memaw's a run for the money."

I glanced at the two strips of bacon resting on my plate and the barely touched grits. Yesterday's incident with Hilda had upset me more than I thought, but not even a murder could dull Candie's appetite.

With a shocked expression on my face, I couldn't help but laugh. "Candie Parker, did you listen to what you just said? Those words would have Memaw reaching for the dreaded wooden spoon. You know she puffed up with pride whenever anyone mentioned her cooking. Memaw claimed she was the best cook in all Hainted Holler, Tennessee. And rightfully so."

My cousin wiggled in the seat and rubbed her bottom. "Ohh, I can feel that spoon making contact with my rear right now."

I smiled. "It didn't happen too often. You outran her old legs most days."

"True. I'd hide out in the barn's hayloft until I knew she'd calmed down." A faraway look crossed my cousin's eyes. "I loved Grandpa's old barn. The fragrant combination of hay and horses—I'll take it over expensive French perfume any day."

"You miss the Holler, don't you?" I prodded.

Candie snapped back to the present. "At times I do. What an innocent part of my life, living with Memaw and Grandpa. I couldn't wait until you came down and spent the summer on the farm. But," she added, shaking her head as if to scatter those memories, "that was then, and now is with you here in Wings Falls. And Mark," she added with a smile.

"Yes, Mark," I repeated. "Did he come over last night after the hook-in?"

"No, we talked on the phone for a little while, but like Hank, Hilda's death kept him tied up." A smile crept across her alabaster complexion. "But he did tuck me in with some good night wishes."

Poor Mark. He was head over heels gaga for Candie. Unfortunately, because of her previous engagements, she suffered from a slight commitment problem. I knew Mark was a keeper. She acted more content than ever before. Happy—yes, she was finally happy. Right down to her ruby-red-painted toenails.

"Oh, there's Jane Burrows." Candie nodded in the direction of the door.

"And her mother," I added, trying to slither under the table. Jane, I could handle. We'd meet up on Monday mornings at The Ewe for our weekly gathering of hookers, and we'd spent yesterday together at the hook-in. Also, I'd frequently used her resources at the library when I researched a particular magazine article I was working on. Usually at the last minute, as I am such a procrastinator, but I do produce my best writing when the promised article is due the next day and I need the check for a designer purse I scoped out on eBay. Or when the cable company threatens to terminate my television usage due to an unpaid bill. Heaven forbid if Porkchop missed a single episode of *It's A Dog's World* on the Animal Planet.

But Jane's mother, Brenda, she was another story. Jane and Brenda practically cloned each other. Both wore khaki pants, spring, summer, fall, and winter. Both sported a collection of button-down-the-front cardigans, and both wore L.L. Bean boat shoes. To top it all off, literally, both styled their hair in a pixie haircut. The only difference? Brenda's hair was snow-white, but Jane's wasn't too far behind. Hers was a mousey brown with strands of gray streaking through it.

Candie waved in the direction of the hostess station.

"What are you doing?" I hissed, tempted to kick my cousin in the shins. But I restrained myself. She'd swear I had crippled her for life. Candie fell into the category of a true Southern Belle and at times was prone to a wee bit of drama, which she will flat out deny.

"I'm only showing the good manners Memaw taught me," she answered back. "You must have forgotten her lesson about being neighborly." Candie huffed and took a compact and a tube of lipstick out of her purse. She flipped open her compact, swiveled up the tube of lipstick, and swiped her favorite, Passion Pink, across her lips.

"You know if they see us, Brenda will want to know all the details of Hilda's death. She won't be happy with what Jane may have told her about what happened yesterday at the hook-in. That woman is a gossip magnet. I don't want to deal with her right now." I drummed the tabletop with my fingers, agitated at my cousin.

Sure enough, within minutes Jane and Brenda stopped by our booth on the way to their table.

"Morning, ladies," Brenda greeted us. She and Jane had unbuttoned the front of their jackets to reveal their cardigans, Jane's a berry red while Brenda's a more subdued olive green. I tucked my legs farther under the table, afraid the knife-sharp crease of their khakis would deal me a deadly blow.

I nodded to acknowledge her greeting then sipped my coffee to keep from having to engage in conversation, something I wanted to avoid at all costs. Brenda's gossip-gathering session could go on forever—until she dragged every last tidbit out of you. I needed to go home and get Porkchop's wardrobe ready for his calendar shoot. My editor had found a local photographer who was able to squeeze Porkchop and me into his schedule. Even though it was a Sunday, the only time he had available was two this afternoon.

The calendar was scheduled for release at the same time as my new book, and hopefully both skyrocketed to big sellers. Doggie outfits covered my den sofa. I'd collected them over the years for Porkchop to celebrate different holidays. Trying to select my favorite was impossible since I thought he was adorable in each one. I loved his pirate hat for Halloween, but the bunny rabbit ears he wore on Easter also ranked up there as a fave. It was particularly adorable when I added a basket filled with doggie treat Easter eggs. Crunch time loomed now. All his outfits needed organizing for the photo shoot.

"I read all about Hilda's death in the newspaper this morning. And of course, Jane here"—Brenda pointed a gnarled finger at Jane—"filled me in on all she had seen and learned yesterday at the hook-in."

At the mention of the hook-in, my mind flipped on alert. I lowered my coffee cup from my lips and asked Brenda, "The newspaper? It's in this morning's edition of the *Tribune*?"

"Yes. Rob Anderson had scored an exclusive interview with Sergeant Peters. It's the big story on the front page. You know Rob, Samantha. He graduated high school with you and is now a reporter for the newspaper," Brenda said.

I nodded in acknowledgment. He may have been in my class, but he had hung with Joe Peters, so we didn't run in the same social circle. Since he and Joe were best buds, it made sense he got the interview.

Brenda held up the first two fingers of both hands as if framing the headline. Squinting her eyes and cocking her head to one side, she said, "The headline read, *Prominent Citizen Dies At Hook-in.*" Then, lowering her hands, she continued, "It should read *The Wicked Witch Is Dead.*"

"She sat on the town council for a while. That's probably why her death has made the headlines. I know you and she had some issues, but don't you think you're acting a little harsh?" I asked. I didn't blame Brenda and Jane for their ill feelings towards Hilda, still they shouldn't speak ill of the dead.

"Harsh!" Brenda screeched. Heads turned in our direction at the sound of Brenda's loud voice. "That woman robbed Jane and me of our family home. I'm sure she lined her pockets with the money kicked back to her from the owner of the dirt bike track. I only hope she didn't profit as much as she thought she would since the venture went belly up a year later."

True, Hilda had sat on the town council and had pushed through a dirt bike track proposal that greatly devalued Brenda's home. A home that had remained in her family for over a hundred years. Speculation had spread at the time. Money may have gone under the table to Hilda to fast track the owner's application. But the venture went broke and closed within a year of opening. None of the allegations had proved true, but the damage was already done. Brenda and Jane were forced out of their home due to the noise and dust created by the dirt bikes. They'd received only a fraction of their home's value.

"I hope the woman died an agonizing death. Tell me, Samantha, did she suffer? It would do my heart good if you told she did," Brenda pleaded.

I sputtered on a sip of coffee. My eyes snapped to the tiny white-haired woman standing next to my booth. Had I heard her right? "Umm, I can't divulge the circumstances of her death. It's privileged police information."

"I guess all of your so-called information isn't so privileged. From what Rob wrote in his article, it sounds like Sergeant Peters considers you the prime suspect in Hilda's death."

My coffee cup slipped out of my fingers and shattered on the table. "What?" I gasped.

Jane, who had stood silently next to her mother all this time, finally found her voice. "Now Mother, you know Sam couldn't do such a thing."

Brenda shook Jane's hand off her arm. "Dear, I don't care if Sam murdered Hilda or not. In fact, I think she'd deserve a medal for ridding this town of that vermin."

Jane tugged on her mother's arm. "Come on, Mother. I think enough has been said. The waitress is motioning us over to our table."

I scanned the cafe as Jane and Brenda moved away from our booth. Was it my imagination, or were the other patrons avoiding eye contact with me?

My cousin, who sat and mopped up my spilled coffee with a handful of napkins, sensed my unease. "No one would believe you killed Hilda."

I only prayed she was right.

CHAPTER THIRTEEN

————

I sat at my kitchen table and sipped a now-cold cup of coffee. I jabbed at the article in this morning's *Tribune* with a half-eaten Pepperidge Farm chocolate chip cookie. "Porkchop, where do Peters and Anderson get off insinuating that I killed Hilda Pratt? I should sue them both for defamation of character or slander or...I don't know, something."

My poor dog cocked his head as he listened to my tirade. He'd suffered through at least fifteen versions of my rant since I had arrived home from my breakfast with Candie this morning. Brenda's account of Rob's, what I considered libelous, article at Sweetie Pie's had fired me up. It had necessitated a stop at the Quickie Mart to grab a newspaper. I needed to read firsthand the offending story in question. My imagination worked overtime. As I paid for the paper, were all eyes in the store staring at me? Was the couple huddled near the slushie bar whispering about me?

I shook my head and crumpled the newspaper into a ball. "Enough of this," I said to Porkchop. "We need to get you ready for your photo shoot. The photographer will be here before we know it." I dumped the rest of my coffee into the sink then pulled out the trash can from underneath. The newspaper went right into the trash where it belonged with the rest of today's rubbish.

"There. It's where it should be, in the trash. Right, Porkie?"

His tail thumped the floor. He probably thought I had asked him about wanting a treat, instead of my opinion of the local rag.

Porkchop's outfits for the calendar shoot needed a few finishing touches. The photographer my editor had hired to take Porkchop's pictures is a fellow named Steve Cruz. I had never met Steve, but that didn't mean anything, as I wasn't familiar with any professional photographers. The only time I'd employed a pro was years ago at my wedding. Since my ex and I had never experienced the patter of little feet, I hadn't needed a photographer's services for the yearly requisite kiddie picture with Santa or the Easter Bunny. It had crossed my mind a time or two to haul Porkchop off to Walmart when they offered their holiday photo package. You know, the one that contained enough photos for your whole family plus every person on your Christmas card list. But in saner moments, I had nixed the idea.

The doorbell buzzed. Who could that be? The only person I expected today was Steve Cruz. I glanced at my watch. It read one o'clock. If it was him, he was early. Both my usual visitors were busy this afternoon, Hank with Hilda's case and Candie working on one of her romance novels. My dog, barking his fool head off, darted to the front door as fast as his stubby legs would carry him.

"Porkchop, hush," I called out, trying to beat him to the door. He may be little, but his bark sounded like a Saint Bernard resided here. I didn't need a security system with his mighty voice announcing everyone who dared to darken my front door. "Oomph, sh—I mean sugar." I stumbled over a foot stool in front of the armchair sitting next to my sofa. I caught myself on the chair before I did a faceplant on the floor.

I peeked out the peep hole in the door and noticed a tall, thin man with his back towards me. My clue that he was the expected photographer, a camera bag was slung over his shoulder. A green rolled-up thingie rested against the railing of my front porch. A large duffel bag sat on the floor next to it. I guessed it was part of his equipment for the photo shoot.

"Porkchop, settle down," I admonished my soon-to-be celebrity pup.

I bent and grabbed his harness while I twisted the doorknob to allow Steve Cruz to enter.

"Sorry Steve, Porkchop thinks he's the guardian to all invaders of his domain." I looked up from my contorted position and gasped. "Where is Steve Cruz? What are *you* doing here?" I straightened and bit back the urge to let Porkchop have his way with the figure who stood in front of me with a grin plastered on his face.

"Hi, Sam. Been a long time. When was it? The last high school reunion?"

"Rob Anderson, not long enough, you low-down snake in the grass. Why aren't you chasing ambulances or cozying up to Sandy Peters?"

He had the decency to blush. "You read my article in this morning's *Tribune*. Pretty good, wouldn't you say?"

My hands clenched. Porkchop yelped. "Sorry, Porkie. I didn't mean to tug so hard on your harness." My temper had risen to the boiling point. I prayed my dog would take a bite out of this insufferable idiot's ankle. How dare he make light of that trash piece he wrote. "You're darn right I did. You wrote a pack of lies. I am not involved with Hilda's murder. I did what any person would do to aide a fellow human in distress. I repeat, why are you here? Or do you finally want the truth about what happened on Saturday?"

Rob tugged on the strap of his camera bag. "Umm… Steve came down with the flu, so he called me to do the photo shoot."

Rob snapping pictures of Porkchop didn't settle well with me. "You… Why you? Since when are you a photographer? My editor wants high-quality images for this calendar. It will be published at the same time as my book."

Rob's right eyebrow rose. "You wrote a book?"

Now my hackles jumped up. Who did he think I was? Some Neanderthal who couldn't put pen to paper? So, I wrote a children's book. In case he didn't know, it's the most difficult genre to get published in. Everyone thinks they can write a kid's book. Little do they know the difficulty in finding a publisher interested in their dear story.

"Yes, I wrote a book, and my editor wants to release a calendar along with it," I gritted out between clenched teeth.

"Cool beans," Rob said. "Anyway, Steve called and asked if I'd cover this gig for him."

"I thought you worked for the *Tribune*." I wouldn't dignify calling him a reporter, not after the article he wrote, insinuating I killed Hilda.

"Yeah, but I took a couple of night classes in photography at the community college, and I'm pretty good if I do say so myself." He plastered a smug look on his face.

I rolled my eyes. *A couple of night classes at the community college!* I took a night class in painting at the local high school a few years ago, but that doesn't mean I'm any Rembrandt.

"Are you going to let me in so I can take the pictures for your pooch's calendar?" Rob bent to scratch Porkchop, who promptly snapped at him.

"Porkie, be good. Sorry, Rob, I don't know what's gotten into him. He's usually so mild mannered." Silently I whispered *good boy* to him. I scooped my buddy up into my arms and swung the door open wider for Rob to pass through into my living room with his equipment.

"I've got his outfits set up in the den. The room's lighting is good in there. It has plenty of windows for natural light. I thought it'd be a great place to take his pictures."

"Lead the way," Rob said. He stood back so I could go before him. "Don't worry about the light. I brought some lights with me that will do the job." He held up the large duffel bag.

A deep growl rose from Porkchop's throat when we passed by Rob. "Hush," I whispered into his ear. "You don't have to like him, but we're stuck for now."

When we arrived in the den, Rob proceeded to set up the green thingie, which he told me was a green screen. When the shoot was finished, my editor could insert any background he wished into the photo. Next, he opened his duffel and pulled out the lighting for taking Porkchop's pictures. I had to admit as the afternoon flew by that Rob might have paid attention in his night classes. He did seem to know what he was doing. Porkchop looked adorable in all his outfits. But I thought the summer shot with him donning a bathing suit, goggles, and a snorkel was the cutest. He'd certainly would have all the girls on the beach drooling for him.

* * *

"How did the photo shoot go?"

It was Monday morning, and only five of us were gathered around the large wooden table in the back room of The Ewe.

For me, it felt like a Vera Bradley kind of day. With the stress of Peters practically announcing to all of Wings Falls that I had killed Hilda, I needed the smile that the happy design of all-over purple flowers on my purse gave me. I placed the purse on an empty chair next to me and pulled my hooking frame out of my red canvas bag then answered my cousin's question. "Good. Rob Anderson took a ton of pictures. Porkchop acted his precious self."

Candie shot me a sideways glance. "Rob? I thought you said it was some guy named Steve."

"According to Rob, Steve came down with the flu. Steve called him to sub at the shoot. I have to admit Rob did look like he knew what he was doing."

"Wait a minute. Isn't this Rob the fellow who wrote that nasty article blaming you for Hilda's death?" Candie's Southern temper wobbled on the verge of erupting.

I stretched my stars and circles pattern over my frame, and with my hook poised over it, I nodded. I needed to finish it before starting the Porkchop pattern Lucy had drawn for me. I tried to discipline myself and not start another rug before finishing the one already stretched across the frame. If I didn't, I'd have a pile of UFOs—unfinished objects. "One and the same. But he doesn't deserve all the blame. He only wrote what Peters insinuated at their interview. He can't help it if Peters is a rat."

"Humph. A good reporter would have gotten your side of the story, too." Candie plopped her frame on the table with a little more force than necessary. To emphasize her displeasure with Rob, I was sure.

"Where is everyone? And where's Lucy?" Usually, at least ten of us sat around the large table on our Monday morning gathering of the Loopy Ladies.

Noticeably absent were Jane Burrows and Roberta Holden, two members who never missed a Loopy Lady gathering. I didn't see Lucy, either. This was her shop, so her presence always filled the room. Ralph sometimes hung in the background, unloading a shipment of wool or some recently arrived order to the shop.

Patsy Ikeda glanced up from her work in progress, a likeness of her Japanese Spitz dog, Hana. I hoped I could recreate Porkchop as well as she was doing with her dog.

"Lucy's been holed up in her office since we arrived about fifteen minutes ago. She got a call on her cell phone and dashed back there. We haven't seen her since," she said.

The two others who gathered around the table, Gladys O'Malley and Marybeth Higgins, nodded in agreement.

Gladys pointed her rug hook in my direction. "I spoke to Roberta earlier, and she said Hilda's passing upset her too much to come today."

I frowned and threaded a strip of wool through my fingers. "How odd. I've never suspected a close friendship between Hilda and Roberta. Yesterday, I considered her a suspect in Hilda's murder."

"It does look a little strange. Especially after Roberta and her husband lost so much money because of Hilda's shenanigans." Gladys dug through a pile of wool strips on the table in front of her.

The sound of sobbing came from the back room. All of us at the table glanced towards the door. A weeping Lucy walked into the room.

I jumped up from my seat and hurried over to her. Lucy shook from head to toe as she fell into my arms. Her body heaved with her deep sobs.

I stroked her back. "Lucy, what's happened? Is it Ralph? Is he okay?"

She gazed up at me. Tears streamed down her lined cheeks. "Oh, Sam, you have to help us. The police... The police," Lucy gulped out between deep sobs.

"Yes, the police?" I prompted.

"They have Ralph."

Lucy collapsed on the floor in a faint.

CHAPTER FOURTEEN

Chairs scraped the scarred oak floor as the other four Loopy Ladies jumped up and ran to Lucy's aide.

Gladys waved us back with her hands. "Girls, step back and give her some breathing room."

I worked to control the smile trying to creep across my lips. I think, being the oldest member of the group, Gladys thought of us as "youngsters."

Everyone retreated a few steps except Gladys and me. I had often dealt with fainting mourners at the funeral parlor, the Do Drop Inn, I co-owned with my ex, George. Lucy needed her feet raised to help with blood circulation. I snatched an armful of folded wool from the hutch next to me then knelt and stuffed them under her feet to elevate them.

"Get me some dampened paper towels." Another Gladys order, but it made sense.

Patsy Ikeda turned, her blunt-cut hair swishing about her shoulders, and rushed over to the deep stainless-steel sink in the back of the room. We referred to it as the dye sink, as we used it to soak yards of wool fabric in water before dying it. She ripped a handful of paper towels from the dispenser over the sink and wet them under the faucet.

When she came back into the hooking room, Patsy handed me the towels. "Here." Worry creased her brow. My gaze roamed about the room and saw the same concerned expression on everyone's faces. A few of the ladies hovered and wrung their hands.

I folded the towels, pushed back Lucy's white bangs, and placed two of them on her forehead.

"Hand me a couple." Gladys extended a gnarled hand towards me.

I gritted my teeth and handed the remaining damp towels to her. Her bossy attitude was starting to wear on my nerves.

I watched as Gladys folded the wet towels and wrapped them around Lucy's wrists.

Lucy groaned. My eyes snapped back to her face. Her eyelids fluttered, and a shaky hand floated towards her forehead.

"What happened?" Lucy asked, pushing herself into a seated position. She grabbed at the paper towels that fell from her forehead. A confused expression clouded her eyes.

I placed a hand under her elbow then helped her to her feet. I guided her over to a chair at the table where only moments before we sat hooking and gossiping. "You must have received some very upsetting news, and it caused you to faint."

Lucy's eyes widened then filled with tears. She pushed a pile of wool strips and a rug hooking frame out of her way. She folded her arms in front of her and placed her head on the table's hard surface. Once again, she dissolved into body-heaving sobs.

I knelt on the floor beside her chair and wrapped my arms around her. My hand did a slow circle over her back in an attempt to offer her some comfort. The other ladies murmured soothing words, too. With raised eyebrows as if to ask *Did anyone know what Lucy meant when she said the police had Ralph?* I glanced from one Loopy Lady to the another. The response was either a shake of the head or shoulders raised in the universal "I haven't a clue" gesture.

"Lucy, what is wrong? Please, we're your friends and want to help. You know we're always here for each other. Remember how you all helped me when I went through my divorce? I couldn't have survived without all of you." My words must have hit a chord, as her sobs started to slow. "Before you fainted, you said something about the police having Ralph?"

She raised her head off the table. Her white hair was now matted with tears. Her mascara, so carefully applied this morning, ran in smudgy tracks down her cheeks. She looked at me then turned to the ladies who sat around the table. "The police—they think Ralph killed Hilda."

Since Lucy was sitting in my chair, I spotted one next to the wall, piled with wool waiting to be shelved. I placed the wool on the floor and pulled the chair up to the table. "You mentioned that right before you fainted. Why do they think he killed her? Outside of her ripping off your designs, you two didn't deal with her, right? Stealing your designs is hardly a reason to kill someone. Get mad, yes, but kill? How ridiculous. What are they thinking down at the station?" I shook my head. Hank couldn't possibly believe Ralph had killed Hilda. But since he was new to the area, he wouldn't know the Fosters as well as the rest of us.

Lucy wrung her hands. "I wish it were as simple as a few stolen designs, but it's more complicated. Ralph's phone call—he wanted the number of our lawyer." She sniffled and reached for the box of tissues sitting in the center of the table. She plucked one out of the box and gave her nose a mighty blow. "Ralph hates, or should I say, hated Hilda."

The Loopy Ladies gasped at Lucy's harsh statement. I even caught myself jerking back from the vehemence in her voice.

"Hate? You and Ralph couldn't possibly hate anyone. You are two of the kindest people we know. Right, ladies?" I nodded at the other ladies sitting around the table.

They in turn answered back, "She's right," along with a few other words of agreement.

I took Lucy's pale hands in mine. "Think of all the wonderful things you do for our community each year. You sponsor food drives for the needy every Thanksgiving and Easter."

Candie tapped the wooden tabletop with a bejeweled finger. "At Christmas you collect toys for less-fortunate children."

"To top it all off, during the summer you send a child from New York City to a camp in the Adirondacks," Gladys added to Ralph and Lucy's list of good deeds.

I nodded in agreement with what my fellow Loopy Ladies had said. "Lucy, your kindness certainly doesn't show me a person who has hate in their heart. Isn't hate a wee bit strong? Like I said, Hilda may have sold a few of your designs. It's not like she killed someone."

Lucy straightened in the chair and swiped her eyes with the back of her wrinkled hands. She glanced at us gathered around the table. "Oh, but she did."

Whats? Whos? Wheres? Whens? erupted from the startled Loopy Ladies' mouths.

My gaze swept the room. "Lucy, what are you saying?" Like all of us gathered around the table, Hilda had lived most of her adult life here in Wings Falls. "I never heard of her being arrested for murder." I shook my head at Lucy's bold statement.

"Let me get a drink of water, and I'll explain the whole ordeal and why my dear Ralph hated her so much."

"You stay put. I'll get you a drink," Candie volunteered. She pushed back her chair and headed towards the sink.

Lucy stared at her hands, wringing them together as she waited for her glass of water. She looked up at Candie and thanked her as my cousin placed a paper cup in front of her. She sipped some water then cleared her throat.

"It all happened years ago. Ralph and I were newly married." A faint smile crossed her lips at that long-ago memory. "We hadn't moved to Wings Falls, yet. We lived downstate. Ralph's mother died when he was a teenager. She left him and his younger brother behind. His father wasn't much help, too broken up by the death of his wife. He drank to deal with the loss of his wife. Ralph had to make sure his kid brother got to school, wore clean clothes, ate, completed his homework. Pretty much everything his mom had done for them."

I choked back tears. My imagination couldn't grasp growing up without my loving parents. I looked at Candie and saw tears teetering on the tips of her eyelashes. She wasn't as fortunate as me. Her parents were killed in a car accident when she was a young girl, but luckily, our sweet Memaw had stepped in and raised her at the family homestead in Tennessee.

Lucy took another sip of water, all eyes trained on her. The rug hooking paraphernalia spread about the table, forgotten. The proverbial pin could have dropped and been the only sound in the room.

Lucy cleared her throat and continued, "Jimmy, he was Ralph's little brother. He went off to college not long after Ralph and I got married. He studied hard and won a scholarship." Pride entered Lucy's voice. "Jimmy wrote us regularly and called about twice a month. Long-distance phone calls cost a lot back then. During one of his calls, he mentioned that he'd found the girl of his dreams."

I glanced at Candie, my romance novel–writing cousin. From the smile on her face, I knew this story tugged at her heart.

"So, what does this have to do with Ralph and the police thinking he killed Hilda?" I prompted.

Lucy's hand curled around the paper cup, squeezing it so hard water spilled onto the table. Patsy jumped up and grabbed more paper towels to sop up the water.

Lucy blinked. "Oh my, I'm sorry. That girl of his dreams was Hilda Pratt. They had dated for about six months. Jimmy had planned to bring her home to meet us over spring break. By his phone calls, he had sounded deeply in love with her, and supposedly she with him."

"So did they come home?" asked Anita Plum. She often dealt with the angst of young love with her own teenage daughters.

Lucy gritted her teeth. "No, Jimmy spent a late-night studying for an exam. Because of his scholarship, he needed to keep his grades up. Hunger hit, so he told his roommate he wanted to grab a bite to eat at the local pizza joint. That was the last time his roommate saw Jimmy alive."

My hand flew to my mouth. I dreaded what Lucy would say next.

More tears streamed down Lucy's cheeks. "You see, when Jimmy entered the pizza parlor, a familiar voice attracted his attention from a booth in the back of the room. Curious, he went to investigate. Curled in another guy's arms and kissing him on the neck sat Hilda."

Again, the Loopy Ladies spoke at once. *The snake! She-devil! Cheater!* floated around the table.

"How could Mari Adams stand her?" Helen Garber asked. She pounded the table with her fist so hard that wool, hooking frames, and hooks jumped. Five heads nodded in agreement.

Lucy's voice trembled. "I couldn't agree with you more and then some. But poor Jimmy became inconsolable. Hilda had stolen his heart and become the love of his life. She's all he wrote of in his letters and gabbed about on the phone. I don't know—maybe he thought he had found in her the love he hadn't received from his parents."

"So, what did he do? Did he call her out on the spot? Break up with her?" the usually quiet Marybeth Higgins asked.

"No. His roommate found him the next morning in the men's room, hanging from a shower curtain rod."

CHAPTER FIFTEEN

———

Silence fell over the small, crowded room. As I gazed about at my fellow hookers, I saw tears flowing down their cheeks. Their hearts broke for Lucy and the unimaginable pain Jimmy's untimely death must have caused her and Ralph.

Lucy sat quietly and twisted a strip of wool around her fingers. I hesitated to speak but needed to ask, "Lucy, his death happened decades ago. Ralph wouldn't wait until now to exact revenge, would he? I know his loss probably still lingers with him, but surely he has adjusted to the tragedy."

Lucy rubbed her hands down the front of her jeans then cleared her throat. "You know how a bunch of guys gather every Tuesday night at Maxwell's Tavern for a game of darts and a few beers?"

"My Charlie joins them once in a while after his shift at the paper mill," Anita Plum said. Her blonde hair, pulled back in a ponytail, swayed back and forth at her excitement to add to the conversation. "I have never said anything about him having a few drafts with his buddies, and he never mentions what I spend on wool."

A faint smile crawled across Lucy's face but faded quickly.

I frowned. What was the connection between a night at Maxwell's and Hilda's death? "So, what does all this have to do with Ralph as a suspect in Hilda's murder?"

Lucy scanned the room. Her blue eyes came to rest on me. "Ever since Hilda started copying my designs, Jimmy's death stabs at Ralph as if it happened yesterday. She accepted no responsibility for his brother's death years ago, and Ralph thought she was mocking us by undermining our business."

I shook my head in disbelief. "Lucy, I can't imagine Ralph involved in Hilda's death. Not your kind, even-tempered Ralph."

The wool strip she twisted in her fingers lay on the table before her in shreds. She gulped back a sob. "A few weeks ago, Ralph drank a few beers too many and got a little loud at the bar. While playing darts, he said he pictured the bull's-eye as Hilda and wanted to stick a dart through her heart. He was loud enough that most of the bar's patrons heard him."

Anita spoke up. "Charlie mentioned it to me, but no one took Ralph seriously. The guys all knew he'd drunk a few too many. People say crazy things when they're a little tipsy." Heads nodded around the table in agreement. "In fact, I think one of the guys he was playing darts with offered him a ride home."

Helen shifted her body in her chair and leaned forward. The large floral print on her blouse strained against her ample chest. "You listen to me, Lucy Foster." Her booming voice commanded attention. All heads swiveled towards Helen. "There's no way Ralph harmed that sorry old Hilda Pratt. I don't mean to speak ill of the dead, but she's made plenty of enemies in Wings Falls. Look what she's done to members of our own little group. She cost Roberta and her husband their life savings, and Jane? Poor Jane and her mom practically gave their house away because of her shady dealings with that dirt bike track owner when she sat on the town council. And her 'BFF' Mari Adams." Helen made air quotes with her fingers. "I'll never understand their relationship. Would you take up with someone if they stole your husband and left you to raise two boys on your own?"

The ladies sitting around the table answered her question in unison with *nope*s, *no way*s, and *when hell freezes over*s."

"You know what I mean? Not many people are strolling around Wings Falls shedding any tears over Hilda's demise. Hear that, Sam!" Helen finished suddenly.

I jerked up in my seat. I was tempted to snap her a salute.

Helen pointed at me. "Make sure your boyfriend starts investigating other people, too."

Heat crawled up my neck. True, Hank and I had been what I considered a couple for a few months now, but it still caught me by surprise when someone referred to him as my boyfriend. It took a little getting used to after abstaining from the dating game since my divorce five years ago. "No need for me to tell Hank how to do his job. I'm sure he's investigating the case thoroughly."

Helen leaned across the table and pointed a chubby finger towards me. "Humph. Use some of your feminine wiles on him," she said as if I hadn't answered. "A little pillow talk will go a long way. And close your mouth. I've spotted his car at your house in the early morning hours. And I'm sure he wasn't doing a police check to make sure you had locked your doors."

I snapped my mouth shut. If I felt heat on my neck before, my face now flamed. Geez, did the whole town know my business? I guess so since Helen knew. She reminded me of the weather alerts that flashed across a television screen as they blared out their message for one and all to know. Beside me, Candie laughed. My smartie pants cousin deserved a kick under the table.

"Ouch," she murmured back at me. Tendrils of auburn hair fell across her face as she reached down to rub the affected shin.

"Lucy, what exactly did Ralph say on the phone? Has he been arrested?" I asked, wanting to get back to his situation.

Lucy shook her head then stared down at her hands. "He wanted Alan Rosenburg's number."

Alan's my lawyer too and acted as my parents' lawyer for years before me. I think he's represented most of the folks in Wings Falls.

"I bet it's standard police procedure and they want to have your lawyer present when questioning Ralph. They only need some information from him because of his and Hilda's history," I said, patting Lucy's arm, wanting to reassure her.

Lucy's watery blue eyes gazed up at me. "Do you think so?" she pleaded.

Crossing my fingers and the toes stuffed into my suede snow boots, I nodded and said, "Sure as I am that Porkchop's calendar will top everyone's must-have list."

A soft laugh escaped Lucy's lips. "Really?"

I pulled Lucy into a hug. "Really."

* * *

Yesterday's meeting with the Loopy Ladies at The Ewe still weighed heavily on my mind. Lucy had called Alan Rosenburg and obtained his counsel for Ralph. It was in their hands now. All the Loopy Ladies could do now for Lucy and Ralph was be there with our moral support, but it still felt like I needed to do more. What, I didn't know…yet. Tonight's dinner out at Momma Mia's, I hoped, would calm some of my fears for Lucy and Ralph.

"Geez, it's colder than a well digger's butt in January out there."

My Southern cousin certainly had a way with words. "My thoughts exactly," I said, rubbing my hands to get their circulation going.

"Hi, Sam. Glad you all ventured out in this weather. Follow me. I saved a table for you away from the door. You won't sit in a draft when it opens. Hang your coats and follow me."

The four of us—Hank, Candie, Mark, and I—did as instructed. Hank helped me and Mark assisted Candie out of our jackets. I'd rather have cuddled in mine for a little longer, but the delicious scents of garlic and tomato sauce circling the restaurant pulled me forward.

We all had dressed to ward off the cold gripping Wings Falls tonight. Style took a back seat when the wind chill hovered in the single digits. Even Candie gave up her filmy blouses for a turtleneck. That wasn't a problem though, since she filled it out better than anyone I knew.

We trailed behind Susan Mayfield, who, along with her husband, owned Momma Mia's, the best Italian restaurant in Wings Falls. It was Tuesday evening, and the restaurant was hopping.

She stopped at a table covered with a red and white cloth and the prerequisite Chianti bottle dripping candle wax down its sides. "How does Lucy feel after our meeting at The Ewe yesterday?"

Susan, a member of Loopy Ladies, found rug hooking a stress reliever from the hectic pace of being a successful restaurant owner. Yesterday, though, was not so relaxing, what with Lucy and Ralph's problems.

"I tried to call her today but didn't get an answer." I sat in the chair Hank had pulled out for me. I smiled up at him. My fingers itched to push back the curl of brown hair falling over his forehead.

Another couple entered the restaurant and claimed Susan's attention. "An insert contains today's specials." She placed four plastic-coated menus on the table in front of us then scurried off to the front desk.

"So, what did Susan mean about Lucy not feeling well?" Hank asked, fingering his menu.

Dean Martin crooned "Volare" as I eyed Hank over my menu. I kept my voice low, only loud enough for him to hear me over the din of the diners. "How did you expect Lucy to feel with your guys grilling Ralph at the police station?" I hadn't seen Hank since Sunday. Seeing Lucy so distraught yesterday still upset me.

"Whoa." Hank put up his hands in defense, trying to shield off my attack.

"I'm sorry. I know you're doing your job." I apologized. "But Lucy and Ralph are good friends."

Hank circled my hand with his and drew me in with his blue eyes, "Sam, I'd expect nothing less from you. Loyalty to your friends is one of the many things I admire about you."

"Umm. Excuse me, but have either of you read the menu yet?" Candie asked.

I blushed and released Hank's hand. My mouth watered as I read over the dinner specials. I poked at my selection on the menu. "I think I'll have a dish of Brian's award-winning spaghetti with his homemade noodles and sauce."

Then I glanced across the table and laughed. "You're one to talk." Candie sat with her head on Mark's shoulder and shared his menu.

"He wanted to point something out to me," my cousin muttered, straightening in her chair.

I grinned and shook my head. "Sure."

Why couldn't my cousin admit she was crazy about Mark? I, along with the whole town, could tell she'd finally found the right guy with the mayor. Maybe having eleven failed engagements made her a little gun-shy.

"Oh, look. Is that Steve Cruz?" Candie asked, nodding toward the photographer who sat two tables over from us.

"He certainly appears to have recovered from whatever ailed him on Sunday," I said, craning my neck for a look at him.

"Oh, I meant to tell you he wasn't sick for Porkchop's photo shoot. Rob Anderson asked for the gig. I think he even slipped Steve a few bucks to let him do it." Candie, who loved all things bling, twisted a large faux-stone ring on her finger.

I felt my blood pressure rising. "How do you know that?"

"Steve stopped by the office this morning to drop off some proofs for Mark's upcoming mayoral campaign. I asked how he was. That's when he told me Rob asked to do your photo shoot."

Mark was gearing up for another run for mayor of Wings Falls.

"I see," I gritted out. So, that snake Rob Anderson wheedled his way into my home on false pretenses. Probably wanted to wrangle a scoop on Hilda's murder from me. Did he think I might spill something about what happened at the hook-in? Poor slob. What a disappointment it must have been. I was too absorbed with Porkchop and his calendar shoot to bother with any of his questions.

"Can I take your orders?"

Pulled back from my thoughts, I didn't notice the arrival of our waitress.

A young girl with olive skin and long black braids that flowed down her back stood next to our table. A name tag engraved with Nancy was pinned to her spotless white blouse. Would it remain white by the end of the evening? If I handled all those sauce-based dishes, I'd be covered in red blotches.

"I'll start. I'm so hungry my stomach could dance on my ribs." Candie waggled her fingers at Nancy. Her jeweled ring sparkled in the candlelight.

I blinked at the brightness of the stone. Its sparkle itched at something in the corner of my brain. That sparkle? What did it want to conjure up?

CHAPTER SIXTEEN

"So, did you like your meal?"

I laughed and nodded at my squeaky-clean plate. "Brian, what do you think?" I asked and pointed at everyone's plates. Brian Mayfield, along with his wife Susan, stood next to our table. He was dressed in his chef's whites and black checked pants. A toque topped his mop of red curls. A satisfied grin of a job well done spread across his face.

Hank rubbed his stomach and groaned. The cream-colored Aran Isle turtleneck sweater I had given him for Christmas rippled under his hand. I smiled as I thought back to his kisses of thanks for his present. We had made proper use of the mistletoe that hung from the archway that led into my dining room. Which led to more kisses on the sofa. Which led to... Well, enough reminiscing or I'd become a pile of Jell-O right here before all of Momma Mia's customers recalling that night.

"Your lasagna even beats my Aunt Gladys's, and she puts together a mean dish of pasta and sauce. But don't you dare tell her. She'd beat me with her wooden spoon," Hank said, shuddering.

Hank's declaration sent all of us into gales of laughter. Gladys was Hank's aunt on his mother's side. Her maiden name was Condi, and she was a true Italian through and through.

Not much terrified Hank, but riling his aunt's temper would make men braver than he quake in their shoes. And Hank ranks as the bravest man that I know, in my unbiased opinion.

Mark tapped his clean plate with his fork. "Best shrimp scampi I've tasted in a long time."

Candie cuddled next to him. She caressed his flannel-covered forearm with her ringed fingers. Again, the rings' sparkle niggled at the back of my brain, but it wasn't clear yet. I smiled. If nothing else, my brain liked the idea of Mark and

Candie as a couple. My poor cousin didn't know it yet, but she'd dropped off the man-hunting market for good.

"Bet you're busy with the incident at the firehouse the other day. It sure has set the town buzzing. It's all my customers talk about." Brian flicked a hand towards the room crowded with diners.

Glasses clinked, silverware scraped his delicious creations off diners' plates, and once again Dino serenaded us with one of his hits. This time "That's Amore" filled the room. Were the heads bent in conversation whispering about Hilda's death and her possible murderer? I hoped I no longer topped their list of possible suspects.

"The gossip spreading around town says arsenic did her in," Brian said, waving to a couple passing by our table.

Hank's eyebrow raised at me.

"Hey, don't look at me. I didn't say a thing," I said in my defense. How the news got out puzzled me, but my lips had remained sealed since Hank had told me—or rather murmured arsenic in his sleep.

Candie sipped her wine, a crisp Chardonnay her choice for tonight, while I preferred my tried-and-true Riesling. The guys had stuck to their beers. "Over a hundred people attended the hook-in on Saturday, so someone's bound to blab," she said, twirling the wineglass in her fingers.

"But who would have known except the police and me?" Mark scratched his bald head. "No one was privy to her cause of death at the hook-in."

"If the police didn't say anything and the mayor's office certainly kept it quiet, who could have blabbed?" Candie asked, licking the last bit of tomato sauce off her fork.

I raised my eyebrows. "What if the murderer let the information slip? On purpose."

Hank sat up straighter in his chair and leaned towards me. Candlelight reflected in his blue eyes. "For what reason?"

"To cast doubt on more possible suspects. Hookers have access to arsenic," I said, running my fingers idly across the checkered tablecloth. I scraped together bits of crumbs from my garlic bread.

"You're right. Didn't a bunch of you ladies take a class from Lucy using arsenic to dye wool a few months ago? I remember Susie went." Brian rubbed his hands together. "All this murder talk isn't good for digestion. How about some tiramisu to round out your meal? Chef's treat."

We all agreed to Brian's generous offer and thanked him. Tiramisu ranked at the top of my all-time favorite desserts list.

After Brian returned to the kitchen, Hank folded his hands on the table and asked, "So what's this about Lucy teaching you and your friends to use arsenic for dying wool? Isn't it a little unusual and rather convenient for her to have the poison used to kill Hilda? It's not like you can walk into your local store and ask for the arsenic aisle."

I gritted my teeth. I didn't like what he had insinuated. "First, you can order it online. Second, it's not unusual. She gave a series of demos on the types of dyes fabric makers used in the eighteenth and nineteenth centuries. Arsenic became a popular dye in the 1800s because it produced a bright green color, unattainable before. It started a rage amongst wealthy women for their gowns. Unfortunately, it also caused a number of deaths. A woman's ball gown could use as much as twenty yards of fabric. Enough particles of the dye floating from her gown, if inhaled, could kill a room full of suitors. If she had any skin abrasions, the arsenic would enter her bloodstream and lead to a very nasty death."

Mark frowned. Wrinkles creased his forehead. "Beats me why you would want to learn about this."

Candie swatted at Mark's arm with her napkin. "Sweetie, we're hookers and want to learn about all types of dying our precious wool."

He rolled his eyes. "I still don't understand."

"It's all right, honey, I know a woman's mind is hard to comprehend sometimes. We do have our ways about us." My cousin batted her long eyelashes at him. She's the only woman I know who could flutter her eyelashes and not look silly.

Hank cleared his throat. "Was Hilda there?"

"Hmm, let me think." We crowded into Lucy's back room. "No, I don't think she was, but others came, not only the Loopy Ladies. Hilda's friend Mari Adams attended. Plus a few others from her group, but I don't know all their names. Oh yes, Mari said Hilda feared she'd have a reaction to the arsenic.

Hilda grew up on a farm, and when she was young, her father used arsenic to keep rats out of their barn."

"Do you ladies have a death wish or something? I mean, why would you risk getting sick or, worse, poisoned?" Mark asked.

"Safety ruled the dye pots in Lucy's kitchen. We wore face masks and rubber gloves. Thank you, dear," Candie said to our waitress, who stood next to our table balancing a tray filled with plates of tiramisu.

Nancy placed a mouthwatering plate in front of each of us. She asked if we needed anything else. When we all said we were fine, she hurried off to help another table of customers.

"Yum," I said. With my eyes closed, I savored the bite of tiramisu I cradled on my tongue. "At least we didn't take Lucy up on her offer to do some dying with poison ivy."

Hank's eyes shot in my direction. "Poison ivy? Man, thinking about it makes my skin crawl," he said, rubbing the sleeves of his sweater.

Laughing, I touched his arm. "We all nixed that. Too many of us react to poison ivy. Besides, it was too late in the season to extract the sap we'd need for dying from the plant's vine."

"The name Loopy fits you ladies to a T. Fooling around with arsenic and poison ivy sounds plain crazy," Mark said, scraping the last bit of tiramisu from his plate.

"But, sweetie, isn't it what you love about me? That little bit of crazy." Candie snuggled closer to Mark.

He blushed. I didn't want to go where I figured his thoughts ran, so I turned to Hank and said, "I think this fabulous meal has made me tired."

As if to prove my point, Candie covered her mouth to hide a yawn. "Sam, I have to agree. Brian's fine cooking made me sleepy as a bear about to hibernate."

Hank motioned Nancy over to our table and asked for the bill. After splitting the total in half and leaving Nancy a generous tip, we gathered our coats from the cloak room, wished Susan goodbye, and then ventured out into the cold night air.

* * *

I sat on my sofa and admired how well Hank's jeans fit his backside. My fingers itched to caress them. He knelt in front of my fireplace and fanned the flames, trying to start a fire. Porkchop lay curled in his bed next to the hearth. I patted the cushion of my sofa and motioned for Hank to join me.

"Thank you for a lovely evening," I said, nuzzling his neck.

He leaned down and turned my face up to his and kissed me. A long, lingering kiss that shot tingles straight to my toes.

My eyes flew open. I jumped off the sofa and ran towards my bedroom. Porkchop, his stubby legs pounding on the wood floor, raced behind me.

"What the...? Sam, what's the matter? Are you all right?" Hank called after me.

True, I could have waited for a better moment to remember what had niggled at the back of my brain, but I needed to show Hank what might become a big clue in Hilda's murder.

CHAPTER SEVENTEEN

I skidded to a halt at my bedroom door. Porkchop didn't put his brakes on soon enough and crashed into my ankles. "Sorry, Porkie." I reached down and scratched between his ears. A room from the past revealed itself when I opened the door. The basket filled with stuffed animals sitting in the corner next to my bed really should go. My bedding was updated, though. A soft gray comforter and pillows replaced the lavender and lace ones from my teenage years. The stuffed Snoopy dog that comforted me all through college now resided in a box in the attic. Although, I did wonder if my Donny Osmond poster hanging over the bed was freaking Hank out. A shopping trip to one of those home decorating stores should be on my to-do list and sooner than later.

I walked over to my maple dresser and flipped opened the jewelry box that sat on top, next to an array of perfumes and lotions. A ballerina wearing a pink tutu sprang into a pirouette and danced to the music of *Swan Lake* when it was opened. The music/jewelry box was a present from my parents on my eleventh birthday. I still remember my delight when I opened the box and discovered my first pierced earrings nestled inside. Candie must have heard my squeal of delight all the way down to Hainted Holler.

I rummaged in the jewelry box and pushed aside my sorority pin from college, a jumble of tangled necklaces, and orphaned earrings. If I ever got the notion to pierce my nose or any other body part, I'll be in great shape. My collection of one-off earrings is large enough for me to wear a different earring every day for a year without a repeat.

"Sam, what are you searching for?" Hank stood framed in the doorway. His broad shoulders filled it out nicely.

"Ouch. This," I said, sucking a fingertip. A pin had jabbed me in my search for the object that I felt was a big clue in Hilda's murder. I untangled the "clue" from a jumble of necklaces.

"What is it? It sure is ugly," Hank said, holding out his hand.

"It's a bracelet that says *hooker*," I said, placing it in his large palm.

Hank flipped it over. "I know, but why would anyone want to wear it?"

"At a hook-in last year, a vendor sold them. A bunch of us Loopy Ladies thought the bracelets would be fun to wear." The rhinestones, spelling out *hooker*, twinkled in the glow from the room's globe-shaped ceiling light.

Hank shrugged his shoulders. A puzzled expression crossed his face. "So, what does this have to do with anything?"

"Hilda," I said, pointing at the bracelet.

Hank frowned. "Yeah, so what about her?"

So caught up in my discovery, I'd assumed he'd know what I referred to. "Like I said, we all bought one of these bracelets at the hook-in. Hilda and her group also attended, and for once they wanted what the Loopy Ladies had and purchased them, too. But Hilda took hers to a jeweler for him to copy into a bracelet of diamonds set into real gold."

Hank let out a low whistle, causing Porkchop to bark. "Sorry, buddy," he said and gave him a pat. "I bet it cost a pretty penny. This Hooker part of this bracelet must be at least an inch and a half long and has what—at least twenty-five stones in it? And that doesn't include the gold in the bracelet. But what does it have to do with her murder?" He examined the bracelet closer.

"Don't you understand? I don't recall Hilda having the bracelet on her arm when she lay dying in the ladies' room. I know she was wearing it because she practically tattooed it on my arm when she rushed out of Lucy's vending area Saturday morning." My state of panic at the time had made everything a blur. "But I did see it earlier in the day when she was at her table surrounded by her friends."

Hanks eyes widened. "You're right. I don't remember a bracelet on her when I arrived in the ladies' room. I would have noticed something this ugly," he said with a grin. "In fact, if I recall correctly, there were scratches and red marks on her wrist."

"So maybe the motive for her murder was robbery. The suspect probably ripped it off Hilda's wrist in haste to remove the bracelet and get out of the ladies' room in a hurry. That's why her wrist was scratched and red," I said. My theory was logical to me.

"How many ladies knew her bracelet contained real diamonds and not paste like yours?" Hank asked. His voice in police mode.

That was an easy answer. "Everyone. She flaunted to everyone who would hear that her late husband had bought it for her."

"Geez, could you narrow the field a little more?" he asked with a chuckle. "Mind if I take this with me?"

"What do you want it for?" It wasn't as if I ever wore it. I had bought it on a whim at the hook-in, caught up in the frenzy of all the other hookers purchasing one.

"Whoever stole Hilda's will want to get rid of it as soon as possible. They probably want to pawn it ASAP. Which one of your hooking friends is strapped for cash?" Hank asked.

I didn't want to point a finger at anyone in particular, so I stalled for time. After all, I might be giving up one of my friends. "Umm, well..." I couldn't look Hank in the face. Bending, I scooped Porkchop into my arms, walked over to my bed, and flopped down. I glanced up at Hank. "Who doesn't need some extra cash every once in a while?"

Hank rubbed a hand across his forehead. "Sam, you're not answering my question." Exasperation at my non-answer laced his tone of voice.

"If I knew someone with a good motive for killing Hilda, I'd tell you." Would I turn in one of my friends? I hoped the puppy dog eyes I shot his way convinced him, because it was hard believing it myself.

"You said whoever took the bracelet would probably pawn it quickly. Where's the nearest pawn shop?" I asked, scratching Porkchop's stomach. He lay on the quilt covering my bed, relishing in my ministrations. My brain spun in search of a pawn shop in Wings Falls. I knew all the local businesses since I grew up here, but I didn't recall seeing any pawn shops. They weren't my go-to places to search out designer purses.

Hank tapped the bracelet with his finger. "It's reasonable to assume that the killer would skip a local shop and head straight to Albany for a wider selection to pick from. She, or possibly he, wouldn't be as easily recognized as in a small town like Wings Falls."

Since I wanted to change the subject in case he returned to the question of who needed money the most, I stood and asked, "Do you want something to eat? A bottle of your favorite beer, Trail's Head, is chilling in the fridge." I could practically see a debate going on in Hank's mind—stay with me or go to the station and start investigating the case of the missing *hooker* bracelet.

Hank drew me into his arms. I nestled into the warmth of his sweater and breathed in the spicy scent of his aftershave.

He heaved a deep sigh. "I wish I could stay tonight, but I better get this bracelet to the station and write up what you told me." He tilted up my head and kissed me deeply. If he hadn't held on to me so tightly, I would have flopped back onto my bed and brought him with me.

* * *

"So, that makes, what, pawn shop number six? Who knew that so many places to pawn your treasures existed?" Candie shook her head and scratched off *Three Golden Balls*, the name of the sixth pawn shop we'd visited, from a pad of paper she clutched in her hand. We had created the list of Albany pawn shops this morning before we set out on this adventure to find the person who stole Hilda's bracelet.

I called Candie last night after Hank left. Like Hank, Mark had made an early night of it, too. Hank had called and given him an update of his findings after he left my house. This murder better be solved soon. It played havoc with my cousin's and my love lives. I had filled her in on our conversation about the *hooker* bracelet and Hank's suspicion that whoever killed Hilda would try to pawn it for money. Now we were traipsing around the city with Candie's *hooker* bracelet, since Hank took mine, and were trying to discover if anyone visited the shops with the likes of the same bracelet.

"Geez. Detecting is killing my feet. I hope we strike pay dirt soon." Candie leaned up against a building, slipped her right foot out of a four-inch-high heel, and reached down to rub the instep and toes of her foot.

"Why did you wear such crazy heels? You could break your neck in them," I scolded.

She stared down at her sore feet then up at me. "When you said we were going to do some sleuthing, I pictured myself as one of those sexy PIs who star in those crime shows on television. They don't have any trouble chasing after the bad guy in their stilettos. Their feet never hurt."

I rolled my eyes and laughed. "Only you, Candie. Only you. Come on, we're here."

"Where?" she asked, slipping her tender foot back into her shoe.

"Look." I pointed to a sign hanging over the door of the building where Candie had sought to comfort her foot.

Candie read the sign that hung over a wooden door. "Pawnography? Seriously? What a name for a store."

I shrugged my shoulders and pushed open the door. The smell of cigar smoke immediately filled my nose. To clear the air, I waved a hand in front of my face. Candie followed behind me and covered her mouth with her hand.

"What's the matter, ladies? Can't handle the smell of a good cigar?" A cackle followed by a deep rattling cough came from behind a glass counter smudged with fingerprints.

I gazed about the store. Metal shelves were filled with electronics, flat-screen TVs, cut glass, what could have been Grandma's silver, and about anything else you could imagine lined the walls.

Candie and I approached the counter from where the cigar comment had come. A gnome-like woman sat in a cushioned rocking chair. She wore an oversized red flannel shirt, baggie jeans, and dirty white Keds sneakers with her pinkie toes protruding out the sides. A lit, half-smoked cigar was clutched between two stubby fingers. Rings of smoke circled her head of frizzy gray hair. Above her hung a framed sign stating in four-inch-high red letters *We're here when you need us.*

"Sounds like something you'd have hung in your funeral parlor," Candie whispered to me. I poked her in the ribs, which got me a glower from her.

"You like the sign? I cottoned to the one hanging there before, but my son, Davie, he didn't think it sounded classy enough. You know, a business like ours that does such a good service for the community and all. The name's Bertha." Bertha rose from her rocker and ambled closer to the counter. If she weighed a pound, she weighed two hundred. As the smoke cleared from where she sat, I noticed a bag of nachos and another of cheese curls sitting on a plastic table, the top crisscrossed with duct tape, next to her chair. A dish full of ashes from her cigar sat next to her snacks.

She held out a pudgy hand dotted with brown age spots. After she shook hands with both of us, curiosity got the better of me and I needed to ask, "What did the sign you liked better say?"

A smile spread across her fleshy jowls. *Daddy sitting in jail? We buy your gold, and you post his bail.* Laughter shook her body. Candie and I couldn't help but laugh along.

Bertha eyed us up and down. "So, what brings you two fine ladies in here today?"

Candie dug in the pocket of her wool plaid coat. She opened her palm and asked, "Has anyone come in to pawn a bracelet similar to this one?"

Bertha's eyes, lost in her fleshy face, widened. She pointed at the bracelet. "It looks like the piece of jewelry the police inquired about earlier."

I swallowed hard. Hank had beaten us here. At least he wouldn't know Candie and I arrived here after him.

"So did anyone try to pawn a bracelet similar to this?" I asked this time.

Bertha squinted at the object of our questions nestled in Candie's palm. "I'll tell you the exact same thing I told those nosy cops."

CHAPTER EIGHTEEN

———

Bertha puffed on the cigar, threw back her head, and blew out a large smoke ring. When she waved the haze away from my face, I stifled the urge to cough. I needed info from Bertha and didn't want to irritate her with my objection to her smoking. She owned the establishment, after all.

Unfortunately, tactfulness isn't one of my cousin's more outstanding traits. "It'll take a month of Sundays to get that smell out of my hair," she hissed out of the side of her mouth.

I glared at her and nudged her side. I hoped she'd get the clue and clam up.

She shot me an innocent look. *What?* she mouthed.

I knew from this past summer, when I tried to prove myself innocent of murdering the owner of the local animal shelter, you got further sweet talking someone than pulling their tail.

I peered into the glass showcase in front of me. "You have a nice variety of items for sale in your shop." The shelves held trays of jewelry: rings, necklaces, watches, brooches, and more. Anything that could possibly have some value. It saddened me to think that some of the objects spread out before me might have been a loving gift from a parent to a child. Maybe to celebrate their graduation or birthday. Even worse, I imagined some of the items were gifts from one lover to another.

I shook my head to pull myself out of my dismal thoughts. "What did you say to the police when they came by?"

"What's it to you gals?" Bertha tapped ash from the tip of her cigar into a glass ashtray resting on the counter. There were several of them strategically placed around the store.

"A friend of mine might be in some trouble. I'm trying to help out." I wanted to divulge as few details of Hilda's death as possible to Bertha.

Bertha tugged at the collar of her oversize flannel shirt. "The cop who came by was tight-lipped, too. And such a cute one. He had the bluest eyes I ever did see."

That had to be Hank.

"Well, Mr. Blue Eyes," Bertha chuckled. "He showed me a bracelet like the one you have there. I told him someone had been in earlier to try to pawn a bracelet like that one there." She pointed to Candie's that lay on the counter. The overhead lights sparkled off the rhinestones.

And... I wanted to roll my hands at Bertha to move the conversation along. But I knew that might cause Bertha to seal her lips. More questions formed in my brain and needed answers.

I wanted to get her back on track. "Could you describe the person you waited on who came in with the bracelet? Was it a man or woman, tall, short, fat, skinny? You know, any info to describe the person?"

Bertha scrunched up her forehead. "You never can tell nowadays. The person wore a beat-up brown puffy coat."

I wrinkled my forehead. "A puffy coat?"

Bertha rolled her eyes as if the village idiot stood before her. "You know, those big down coats we all wear this time of year to keep Old Man Winter from freezing our asses off."

I nodded. "Right. So, anything else you remember about the person?"

"Hmm, let me see. I guess she—and if I scratch my memory, I'd say I'd lean to the person being a she—didn't look too tall. Then again, I'd say she wasn't too short either. Sort of average, I'd say. I told the cops the gal wore large sunglasses. A wool cap covered most of her hair. She'd draped a scarf around her neck. It came clear up to her chin." Bertha rolled the cigar between her fingers.

"Was the person old, young, have long or short hair?" Candie startled me when she chimed in. I thought she was too busy eyeing the baubles in the showcase to pay attention to my conversation with Bertha.

"Like I already said, her coat pretty much covered her up. Oh, yeah, I do remember some long, stringy brown hair escaped from the cap."

I mentally absorbed everything Bertha had said. "Sounds as if she didn't want to be identified."

"Well, she's narrowed the field down," Candie mumbled beside me.

I resisted the urge to kick her. One thing about my beloved cousin, keeping her mouth shut was a difficult task. You always knew where you stood with her. A good trait, but one I wished she kept to herself right now. I tapped on the showcase next to us. "Why don't you check out those rings? Maybe one will strike your fancy and Mark can buy it for you."

"You don't have to drop a sledgehammer on my head. I'll be quiet from now on, but maybe I will check those sweet little ol' rings out. One of them might be calling to me to take it home."

Candie sidled down the counter a few paces while I thought of my next question for Bertha. "How much did you value the bracelet?" I unzipped my coat. It might be cold outside, but Bertha had cranked up the heat to a subtropical temperature.

"Worth a pretty penny if you ask me." Bertha jabbed at Candie's bracelet with a stubby finger. "It looked like your friend's here, but hers is only paste. Worth maybe, on a good day, ten bucks."

Candie's head flew up from concentrating on the rings in the case next to us. "What? It cost me twenty-five."

Bertha shrugged her rounded shoulders. "Gal, I ain't no charitable organization. I got to make a buck. Anyways, why would you ladies of the street want to advertise what you're doing wearing such jewelry?"

Candie's back stiffened. In two strides her high-heeled shoes brought her next to me.

Oh, geez, here it comes. Dear cousin had her dander up.

She pointed a manicured finger at the bracelet. "I'll have you know I am a well-bred Southern lady. That bracelet stands for a hobby of mine—rug hooking. I am not, as my Memaw Parker would say, a lady of the evening." Having said her piece, she stomped back to eyeing a tray of rings.

Bertha stood wide-eyed staring after Candie. "Sorry. Didn't mean to rile you up, but in this here part of town you can find those 'ladies of the evening' on about every street corner."

I needed to diffuse the situation and turned my attention back to Bertha. "Your mistake is understandable. It's an inside joke we rug hookers share. Sounds a little naughty calling ourselves hookers."

I wanted to get us back to the reason for our visit— identifying Hilda's murderer. If we could discover the person who ripped the bracelet off Hilda's wrist, we'd have our killer. After all, greed ranked, along with jealousy, as one of the leading reasons for killing someone. I didn't know who'd be jealous of Hilda. Yes, she rubbed several people the wrong way. No, I corrected myself, she irritated a lot of the people in Wings Falls, but over the years most people ignored her. Apparently, though, she'd gotten under someone's skin enough for them to want to kill her. "The bracelet our mystery person brought into pawn—was it worth anything?"

"Worth anything?!" Bertha bellowed. Candie's head whipped around at Bertha's loud voice. "Sweetheart, with all those diamonds set in gold, that chick's bracelet cost a fortune, and real fine quality, too."

"So, it's worth…?" I let the word drag out, figuring she'd say a few thousand dollars, tops.

"At least ten thousand," she said.

Candie scooted over to my side faster than snow could melt on a stove top. "Hush your mouth. Did you say ten thousand dollars?" she gasped.

I reached up and closed my cousin's dropped jaw.

Curious now as to how the mystery woman reacted, I asked, "So, what kind of offer did you make to the woman?"

Bertha's hand hovered over her cigar in the ashtray. "I told her I'd give her five thousand cash, right then."

"Did she take you up on your offer?" I asked. Trying to drag info out of Bertha wasn't easy.

"She acted real insulted. She said I tried to rob her with such a low offer and she wanted to check out what my competition would give her. She stomped out the door in a real huff."

"It does sound a little low," I said.

"What do you take me for, Santa Claus? If you ladies don't want to buy anything, I've got work to do." Bertha turned and walked through a doorway covered with a pair of shabby curtains.

Back out on the street, the sun had turned the snow from this past weekend into slush.

"Geez, touchy," Candie said. She peered through Pawnography's window. "If she'd acted nicer, I saw a ring I thought needed to come home with me." She held out her right hand and wiggled her ring-ladened fingers. "I can see it right there wanting to join its friends." She pointed to her index finger. "I'm hungry. Let's stop some place to eat."

I nodded, and the two of us headed back to my car. As I shoved my key into the Bug's ignition, something Bertha had said struck me. "Candie, Bertha said the woman, and I'm assuming now it was a woman, who tried to pawn Hilda's bracelet wore a knit cap, but some of her hair escaped it. 'Long, stringy brown hair,' she said."

She looked up from fastening her seat belt. "Yes, so?"

"Don't you see? Lucy's hair is white. Jane Burrows sports a short brown hairdo, and Roberta bleaches her hair blonde."

Candie's mouth formed an "O." A light bulb had flicked on in her head, too.

CHAPTER NINETEEN

———

"Hold that thought. We'll ponder it over lunch," I said, nodding. "Do you know of any place to eat around here?" I had never been in this part of the city. I scanned the area for an eatery I hoped wouldn't serve up food poisoning with their burgers. The snow, which was once a gleaming white, clung to sidewalks. It was covered with dirt and soot. Empty beer cans, crumpled paper, and discarded cups from the nearest coffee shop littered the street curbs. March marked an ugly time of the year in the North Country.

My cousin shook her head. "Honey, my taste in dining may be simple, but Mark would stand in line as another ex if he took me to dinner around here."

A few minutes of driving saw us in a greatly improved neighborhood. At least the streets were a little neater, if they counted as a judge for what the local dining establishments offered.

"There! Over there... That diner across the street looks inviting." Candie pointed a ringed finger at a silver-clad building flashing a neon "open" sign in its window. "Besides, my stomach is about shriveled up. I don't think I'll survive much longer if I don't eat something and soon."

I smiled. Candie had missed her calling. She should have trod the boards on Broadway. Instead she earned her living as a secretary and romance writer.

"Okay, I don't want to be the one who has to call Mark and tell him you've perished from starvation. By the way, what did he say when you wanted a few hours off this morning?" I glanced at the Bug's digital clock. Noon was well past taking a few morning hours off from work.

My cousin tucked a stray curl behind her ear. "I've worked a bunch of overtime lately. I'm owed a few hours off.

The town's budget is due soon, so I stayed late a couple of days to help Mark organize it."

A happy feeling spread inside me. Candie was fast becoming an integral part of Mark's life, both personally and professionally.

A packed parking lot sat to the side of the diner. I turned the Bug into the lot and looked for a vacant space. "Do you think we can eat here? There's no place to park," I lamented.

"Wait!" Candie pointed to a couple in front of us who walked to a tan Ford Escape SUV—at least I think it was tan, since road salt covered the lower half of the car. A shot of cold air rushed in as she lowered her window. "Yoo-hoo, are you leaving?" she shouted to the man and woman. Candie leapt out of the Bug when the fellow nodded a reply to her question. My mouth hung open as she waved the couple's car out of their slot and motioned for me to take its place. Beware if anyone had dared to delay my cousin's lunch a moment longer than necessary.

* * *

"It's not that funny. How else do you think we'd get a parking space if I didn't take action?" Candie asked, scowling at me.

I stifled a laugh that wanted to escape my lips. I had been laughing since we entered the diner. I sat back in my seat and took in the decor. While not as freshly painted or as nicely decorated as Sweetie Pie's, the place was clean. If the food tasted as delicious as the desserts tempting me from under a plastic dome on the counter we had passed on the way to our table, we wouldn't be disappointed. Caught in a time warp, sun-faded posters that advertised ice cream sundaes, hot dogs, and soda decorated the diner's walls. A chalkboard behind the counter stated the daily specials. Today's special—a deluxe burger and fries for $4.99. My stomach's juices awoke with a resounding growl.

Candie's head popped up from behind the menu that the waitress who sat us had placed on our table. "Did you say something?" she asked.

I chuckled. "No, but my stomach did." I pointed to the chalkboard. "I think I'll have the daily special."

Candie nodded. "That sounds good to me."

I motioned for our waitress, and we gave her our orders. To complete the order, we added chocolate milk shakes to the burgers and fries.

We settled back into the booth and waited for our lunch. "So, what idea popped into your head when I mentioned the color of the lady's hair?"

Candie leaned across the chipped Formica table. In a hushed voice, she said, "Bertha said long, stringy brown hair had escaped from under the person's hat who came in with the bracelet"

"Right. So, did you come up with the same conclusion as me?" I asked her in a low voice. True, people jammed the diner and engaged in their own conversations. The din of clanking silverware on heavy porcelain plates filled the room, but I wouldn't take any chances that we'd be overheard.

"It couldn't be Lucy, Jane, or Roberta because none of them have long brown hair. Also, Ralph's out as a suspect since Bertha thinks a woman wanted to pawn the bracelet," Candie said, drawing circles on the chipped Formica tabletop with her scarlet fingernails.

Our waitress arrived with our lunch order. "Here you go, ladies." She balanced a large tray on her shoulder while she placed the milk shakes and platters of burgers before us.

I inhaled the fragrance of our burgers. "The aroma of a freshly grilled hamburger outdoes any French perfume in my book. I bet if I could bottle it, I'd make a million dollars."

Candie laughed. "If nothing else, you'd have every dog in town nipping at your heels."

I munched on a crisp French fry. "Yeah, that would be a downside, and I don't think Porkchop would be in favor of a hoard of dogs vying for my attention. He'd be jealous with a capital J. He demands my undivided attention."

"How does Hank handle it when he's at your place?" Candie sipped her milk shake.

I shook my head and twirled another fry in the ketchup I had squirted on my plate. "It's funny. When I was married to my ex and Porkie sat next to me, he'd growl if George came too close. But he loves when Hank comes over. His tail doesn't stop wagging—Porkie's, I mean. Not Hank's."

"That sounds like a traitor if you ask me," Candie said between bites of her hamburger.

"No, I'd say the dog has good taste. But back to the woman who came into the pawn shop. What if she wore a wig? She certainly was trying to hide her identity underneath the big coat, hat, and scarf she wore."

Candie's burger stopped midway to her mouth. A frown creased her forehead. "You're right, so that would mean Jane, Roberta, and Lucy should still remain on our suspect list. But do you think they wanted to kill Hilda?"

I sipped my milk shake and nodded. "They all had a reason to kill her. Lucy lost a good deal of money by Hilda pirating her designs. Jane and her mother practically gave their house away when Hilda, as a member of the town council, helped get the dirt bike park approved. Roberta and her hubby also lost a great deal through Hilda's bad investment advice. And let's not forget Lucy's husband, Ralph."

"Ralph? But Bertha says the person was a woman. Wouldn't that eliminate Ralph?" Candie asked.

"Everything fine, ladies?"

So absorbed in our conversation, I hadn't noticed our waitress approach our table. "Fine. These are delicious burgers. My compliments to the chef," I said, pointing to my plate now clean of any food.

The waitress laughed. "Don't know if I'd call Pete a chef, but I'll pass your message along. It'll make his day." She cleared our table of the empty plates and asked, "Any dessert, gals? Got some delicious homemade banana cream pie. Fresh made this morning."

I shook my head and eyed my cousin. "I couldn't stuff another morsel in me."

Candie groaned and agreed. "None for me, either. I'll be splitting my corset stays if I try to take another bite. Sure tasted delicious, though, sweetie."

Our waitress finished clearing the table and said she'd be back in a few minutes with the check.

Candie pulled her wallet out of her purse. "Why would you suspect Ralph? Clearly he wasn't at Pawnology."

I dug through my gray faux leather Michael Kors for my wallet, too. I loved the long strap on my handbag. It made it convenient to sling the purse over my shoulder. "What if Lucy wanted to protect Ralph and convinced him to let her take the bracelet to the pawn shop? He certainly had motive. After all, his brother had killed himself because Hilda cheated on him."

"Hmmm, interesting," Candie said.

Yes, very interesting.

* * *

"Geez, when is spring going to come?" Candie asked, clapping her mittened hands together.

"It can't get here soon enough," I said as we crossed the crowded parking lot to my car. "What a delicious burger, though. I'm stuffed."

"I'd better get back to work. I may date Mark, but he's all business at the office," Candie said, walking next to me.

"Yeah, I've got a Friday deadline to meet. I'm writing an article about Doctor Rene Theophile Hyacinthe Laennec. Did you know while observing a group of children play on a pile of boards, it inspired him to invent the stethoscope?"

Candie rolled her eyes at me.

"Okay, so I don't write your heaving-breasts style of books, but my articles put money into the bank, too," I said, defending my writing.

Candie grabbed my arm, stopping me in mid-stride. "Sam, what's wrong with the Bug?"

I looked in the Bug's direction and noticed it leaned to one side. I hurried over and stopped short next to the driver's side.

Candie caught up to me and gasped. "Someone slashed your tires."

CHAPTER TWENTY

"Who would do this?" My body shook with rage at the sight of my deflated tires.

"Probably some punk kid out for a few laughs." Candie pulled her bejeweled cell phone out of her purse.

"Yeah, ha-ha, the joke's on me." My shoulders sagged at the cost of two new tires. I guess the new Louis Vuitton I'd drooled over online would have to wait for another day.

"Yes, ma'am. I want to report an act of vandalism to my friend's car. Uh, hum, some nasty person slashed my cousin's car tires. You'll send an officer right away? Honey, you're so sweet."

I snapped out of my funk as my cousin gave the person on the other end of the phone our location. "Thanks. I wasn't thinking clear enough to give 9-1-1 a call. I better call AAA, too. It may take them a while to get here. Geez, the tow charge will cost me a fortune." I scrolled through the contact list on my phone and punched the number for AAA. I only had their basic coverage plan, and at the thought of the bill, I knew I'd be lucky if I could afford another designer purse by the time I checked into Sunny Hills Retirement Home.

"Lookie, it must be the police." Candie pointed to a black Chevy Impala that pulled into the parking lot. "They drive such plain Jane cars. Now, if it was up to me to pick the color for their squad cars, I'd spice things up some with a glittery purple or maybe baby blue like my Precious."

I rolled my eyes at my cousin's suggestions, but I was amused. If nothing else, life sparkled when we hung together. As the car pulled up to us, my sense of relief turned to dread. I recognized the officer behind the aviator rimmed sunglasses that sat in the passenger seat.

"Oh, goodie, it's Hank." Candie waggled her fingers at him.

"Don't tell him about our mission here," I hissed out of the corner of my mouth.

Hank's lanky form emerged from the car. "Hi, Sam, Candie."

I waved a mittened hand in greeting and responded with a weak, "Hi."

"You know these ladies, Hank?" A gentleman joined him. I assumed he was a fellow detective, since like Hank he wore street clothes.

"Charlie, meet Sam Davies and her cousin, Candie." Hank strode over to my Bug. He crouched down to assess the damage to the car's tires.

"Hello, ladies. I'm Charlie Perkins, Hank's old partner before he left us and moved to the North Country." Charlie reached out a large hand and enveloped mine and then Candie's in a handshake. I'd thought Hank was tall at 6'2", but Charlie beat him by at least three inches. His rumpled trench coat reminded me of the old television show detective, Columbo. All he was missing was the half-smoked cigar dangling from his fingers.

I switched my attention from Charlie to Hank. "What brought you to Albany? Shouldn't you be in Wings Falls?"

He stood and walked over to me. A chill wind whipped up and stirred the trash littering the parking lot. People on the way to their cars stopped and stared at the four of us. A few pointed and whispered amongst themselves about my poor Bug and its lopsided condition.

"I'm thinking the same thing about you and Candie, Sam. Aren't you a long way from home?" Hank asked.

I glanced at Candie and nudged her foot, trying to send a silent message. I prayed she wouldn't spill the beans about our real purpose in this not-so-glamorous side of Albany. "Um, I read about a designer purse sale in a little boutique a few blocks from here." Words rushed out of my mouth. My hands broke out in a sweat inside my thick mittens. I am a lousy liar.

Hank's right eyebrow arched up. "What was the name of this boutique having the purse sale?"

Great, caught in my own lie. "Umm, Purse Heaven or something like that, but Candie got hungry, so we stopped here for a bite to eat." I motioned with my head towards the diner.

Hank pointed to my shopping bag–free arms. "No luck in finding a new purse?"

Drat. Why did he have to be such a good detective? Heat crawled up my neck as I mumbled, "No. No luck."

Candie jumped into the growing awkward silence. "Sam's right, Hank. I was hungrier than a coon dog sniffing out a possum. And you know me, if hunger calls, I need to feed that little devil. After we left the boutique, I saw this cute little diner and insisted Sam pull in here or I might perish. You wouldn't want her to have to tell Mark about my untimely demise from lack of nourishment. Now, would you?" Candie fluttered her eye lashes and stuck her Passion Pink covered lips out in a pout.

Charlie, who had stood next to Hank but remained silent, chuckled. "Well, ladies, you picked a great place to eat. Hank and I used to stop at Pete's Diner whenever we cruised the area."

"So, what brought you here, Hank, and how did you know I needed help?" How did my misfortune cause him to respond to our 9-1-1 call?

"Since Charlie and I used to work this part of the town, I called in a favor and asked if he'd help me canvas some of the pawn shops that populate this section of town. I figure whoever killed Hilda and ripped the bracelet off her arm needed to get rid of it and fast. In a larger city, it's less likely they would run into someone who knew them," Hank said.

"Um, that makes sense to me. Glad you thought of it," I said then wanted to do a palm plant on my forehead. Of course, he'd think the murderer would go to a big city. He's a detective, and it's his job to check out all angles. I'm sure he's done this a million times.

A large tow truck rumbled into the parking lot. "Must be the AAA," I said, reaching into my purse to get out my membership card to show the driver.

"Hi, folks. Someone here need my help?" the driver asked as he ambled towards us. Oscar's Garage was embroidered in red thread over the right breast pocket of his heavy blue canvas jacket. A grease-stained Yankees ball cap sat on his head. Black grease was the main color of his denim overalls and scuffed work boots.

I pointed to my poor Bug. "It would be me."

"Geez, someone sure must not like you, lady. What a rotten thing to do. By the way, I'm Oscar." He rubbed a day's growth of whiskers on his chin with a gloved hand.

"Yeah, rotten," I repeated, showing Oscar my card so he could proceed with loading the Bug onto his truck for the long and expensive trip back to Wings Falls.

"Do you want me to tow it to a local garage?" Oscar asked as he climbed back into his truck.

"No, I've got a guy in Wings Falls I've used since I was a teenager," I said and gave him the address of the garage where I wanted it towed.

"That long, huh?" Oscar said, leaning out his truck window as a thick wire cable pulled the Bug up onto his truck.

I bristled at Oscar's remark. "He makes me feel ancient," I mumbled to Candie.

As the tow truck retreated out of the parking lot, Charlie said, "I'll check with Pete for access to his security camera."

"Security camera?" I asked, scanning the parking lot.

Hank pointed to the corner of the diner. A small camera-type device was mounted near the roof of the building.

Candie clapped her hands. "Oh, goodie. We'll be able to catch the thug in the act."

"Don't get your hopes up, ladies. More often than not the owners don't keep them activated. Too much of a hassle for them," Charlie said and walked towards the diner's entrance, leaving Candie and me standing next to Hank.

"So, want to fess up, Sam? Your trip here wouldn't have anything to do with Hilda's murder, would it?" Hank asked.

I bit the inside of my cheek. *How could I answer him without outright lying again? I wasn't good at it, and I suspected that he knew it.*

"Hilda's murder certainly bothers me. How could it not? Sergeant Peters wants to pin the murder on Ralph. He probably thinks Lucy planned it, too. He must think they're a modern-day Jack the Ripper and Lucretia Borgia. Heck, he would arrest me if he could. Does he think we're a gang of murderers on the rampage?" I asked, trying my best to avoid directly answering his question.

"Joe means well, even if he does act a little overzealous," Hank said, pulling a pair of leather gloves out of his tweed overcoat. A frigid wind whipped through the parking lot

"Overzealous?" I repeated. "Don't you remember last summer when the owner of the animal shelter was killed? He wanted to lock me up and throw away the key."

"I do, but everything worked out for the good," Hank said.

Now my feathers were ruffled. "And if you remember it's because of my investigating that I discovered the murderer."

"Yes, but in case you forgot, you were almost shot by the suspect. I don't want anything to happen to you, Sam. Murderers are often desperate people. They want to avoid capture for their crime." Hank stared into my eyes with a pleading look.

I swallowed hard. "I'll be careful, Hank. I promise." It's all I would concede. I wouldn't abandon my friends.

"I guessed right. Pete said his security camera hasn't been checked in months. Too much of a hassle."

Candie and I both jumped at the sound of Charlie's deep voice.

My cousin's hand fluttered to her chest. "Honey, you about scared me right out of my boots."

Charlie chuckled. "Sorry, ma'am."

"Not much more for us to do here. Come on. We'll take you back to the station where you can sign the complaint and we can file it. Unfortunately, I doubt if we'll ever find out who did this. We're done for the day. When you're finished at the station, I'll give you a ride back home." Hank moved towards the Impala.

"Oh, I've never been in the back of a police car before," Candie said, taking in her surroundings as we climbed into the car.

"Wasn't fiancé number two a deputy on Hainted Holler's force? Didn't he ever show you his squad car?" I asked, snapping on my seat belt.

Candie's face turned red. "How could I forget about Johnnie Boy? He did carry some big guns."

"I'm sure he did," I said, laughing.

My cousin leaned over to me and whispered, "I've thought about what the tow truck fellow said, and I'm a wee bit worried."

My head snapped up. Not too much worried my carefree cousin.

"What if the person who slashed your tires did it deliberately?" she asked.

"You're silly. How would they even know we were in Albany?" I asked.

I shivered. *But was Candie's concern really so silly?*

CHAPTER TWENTY-ONE

———

"Porkchop, I haven't thawed out yet from my chilly ride home from Albany yesterday. If Hank had clenched his jaw any tighter, I swear it'd snap." I sat on my den sofa with my Porkie curled up next to me. My rug hooking nestled on my lap with a third morning cup of coffee on the end table beside me. I didn't know what registered colder yesterday after Candie's and my aborted adventure to pawn shops in search of clues to Hilda's murderer—the air inside Hank's squad car or the brisk March air whipping around us outside. The only thing to make the ride home bearable was Candie chattering on in the back seat about the squad car itself. She'd wanted to know the purpose of various knobs and switches on the front console. She'd tried her best to get Hank to flip on the siren, but to no avail.

Porkchop cocked his head as if he absorbed every word I spoke and with great understanding. Hooking always calmed my jumping nerves. The mindless pulling up of wool strips zoned me out. After yesterday's adventure and Hank's displeasure about Candie's and my activities, I wanted to clear my mind. I needed to sort out what we'd learned on our trip to the big city. Porkchop acted as the perfect sounding board. "Porkie, here are the facts—someone killed Hilda and in a very gruesome manner. Unfortunately, I believe a hooker performed the deed, and it was, most likely, someone I know. They obviously carried a grudge against Hilda." My pup let out a low growl. "Yeah, I know, that could be half of Wings Falls," I said, scratching him behind the ears. I must have hit his sweet spot, as his left hind leg started to thump the sofa cushion.

"The most obvious suspects are Ralph, Lucy, Jane, and Roberta." I frowned. "There has to be someone else. Even though she did some terrible things to them, I can't believe they would murder Hilda." A shiver ran down my back. "But you know, Porkchop, some very nice people have been known to do terrible things."

To scatter these disturbing thoughts from my brain, I set to hooking again. I reached into the basket holding my colored wool strips for the pattern stretched across my rug hooking frame.

I had finished the rug I worked on at the hook-in—the patriotic runner of stars and circles. It was draped over the trunk in front of my sofa. My current project was the pattern of Porkchop Lucy had drawn up for me. I poked around the basket, searching for more reddish brown for his body.

"Drat, Porkchop, I don't have any more of the wool for your body. That's what happens when you hook your strips as close as I do," I said, sifting the strips through my fingers. Hooking my rows tightly was a bad habit I had developed over my years of hooking and couldn't seem to break. Early on, when I learned how to hook, I was told that my rows should "hug and not kiss," a rule I'd never mastered. I took mental stock of the browns stashed on a shelf in my basement craft room. Nope, I concluded none of them would do. I laid my hook on the end table and glanced out the front picture window. "Porkchop, how about we take a walk to Lucy's shop?"

He jumped off the sofa and beelined it to the front door. I suspected he knew Lucy kept a jar of treats reserved for him under her counter, and with his HERSHEY brown eyes, he could hit Ralph up for a rawhide bone.

"I'm sure she's open by now," I said, peeking at my watch. "Geez, practically noon. Where did the morning go?"

* * *

The walk of two blocks to The Ewe took less than ten minutes, even with stops along the way for Porkchop to sniff every nook and cranny. The morning sun warmed us on our walk. None of the biting wind from yesterday. Maybe spring would arrive soon. I could only hope.

"Now be good, Porkie," I said, pushing open the wooden door to Lucy's shop. My fingers itched to dig into a pile of wool stacked on the shelves circling the room. The rainbow of colors dancing before my eyes always brought me to a happy place. A sense of calm settled over me. The stress of yesterday's adventure seeped out of my body.

"Lucy," I called out. She wasn't in the front room of the store. Porkchop joined in with a bark. "Hush," I reprimanded him.

Laughing, Lucy emerged from her back room. She peeled off a pair of rubber gloves. "Ahhh, two of my favorite people," she said, bending to pat Porkchop. Lucy always said he acted more human than dog, smarter than some people she knew, too.

"Treat, Porkchop?" Lucy asked. He answered with another bark and a tail wagging at super speed. Lucy walked over to her counter and pulled out a glass jar full of bone-shaped snacks she kept tucked underneath.

"What a morning. The Loopy Ladies are busy pulling loops," Lucy said, joining me after replacing the treat jar under her check-out counter.

"Really?" I asked, curious to know who else needed to satisfy their hooking cravings.

"Yes, both Jane Burrows and Roberta Holden stopped in earlier. They wanted wool for their projects. Thankfully, I could fulfill their needs."

Porkchop sat at her feet and gazed up with sad eyes. He probably hoped for another treat, but Lucy knew she should give him only one or he'd roll into her shop instead of prancing in like he owned the place.

"Guess, I'm right behind them. I don't have enough wool to finish Porkchop's body in the rug you designed for me. You know how tightly I hook. Do you have any more?" I pulled my rug pattern out of the canvas bag slung over my arm.

Lucy excelled in color planning. All of us Loopy Ladies depended on her to give our rugs the right touch to make them pleasing to the eye.

"Let me check what I've got back in the dye room. I slaved over the dye pots this morning. Afraid I couldn't give Jane and Roberta much attention when they came in. They made out fine, though. Both went home with a bundle of wool."

I laughed. Wool became an addiction to rug hookers. We never could own enough. "I'm sure they helped each other out," I said, wandering over to a shelf of wool.

"No. They came in separately, Jane before the library opened and Roberta about an hour later," Lucy said.

"Oh, I assumed they arrived together. They are close friends." Like many crafts, hooking formed close ties amongst friends.

I spread my pattern on the long oak table situated in the center of the room. "So, what do you think, Lucy? Do you have more of this wool available?" I pointed to Porkchop's almost finished body.

"Hmm, let me think. Come back to the dye room. I cooked up a fresh pot of reddish-brown wool this morning. Let's see if any of them will match Porkchop."

Like Porkchop salivating over a juicy bone, I trailed after Lucy into the small room off her studio. She worked her magic here, creating rainbows of dyed wool. As I walked through the door, a stainless-steel sink faced me. A well-used electric stove and a dryer lined the wall to my left. A dye-stained Formica counter separated the dryer and stove. A stack of brown wool lay folded on this counter. But not any old brown. Browns from walnut brown to deep M&M's brown.

"How about this?" Lucy asked, pulling out a piece of wool from the pile.

My eyes widened. A smile crept across my face at the reddish-brown fabric Lucy held up. I fingered the wool. "Perfect. Lucy, you are a genius—or, should I say, magician. Or maybe both? You created what I need to finish my sweet Porkchop."

Lucy's white hair bounced about her shoulders as she laughed. "I don't know about being a magician, but I love to mix up my color potions and discover what I can create. It does feel like magic at times. Sometimes I never know what will come out of the pots."

"A real adventure, putting a little of this color and a little of another together and never knowing the end result." I glanced at the shelf above her counter. A row of jars containing dye colors lined it. At the end of the row sat the bottle of arsenic she used in her dye class on colors in the nineteenth century.

"Lucy, has Sergeant Peters questioned either you or Ralph any more about Hilda's murder?" I asked, hoping he no longer suspected her or her husband of Hilda's death.

Lucy nervously fiddled with the stack of wool. She folded then refolded the pieces of wool. "No, thank heavens. We hope he's discovered clues to lead him to suspecting someone else other than us."

The bell over the shop's door chimed. Porkchop barked.

"I'll be right out," Lucy called to the newcomer.

"No hurry, Lucy. I'll look around," the person called back.

My eyebrows lifted in inquiry. *Mari?* I mouthed to Lucy.

Lucy shrugged. We reentered the studio to satisfy our curiosity.

"Hi, Mari," we both said at once. I tried to hide my surprise at seeing her. Because they didn't belong to the Loopy Ladies, Mari, Hilda, and their group of hooking friends usually ordered their supplies off the internet. Me, I preferred to check out my wool in person. Since Lucy and Ralph became suspects in the murder of her best friend, why would she patronize The Ewe?

Laughing, Mari responded, "Hi, ladies. Such a sweet doggie. What's his name?" She scratched him behind his ears.

My dog leaned into her hand. "Porkchop," I answered.

"What can I help you with?" Lucy asked.

"I want to hook a rug in honor of Hilda. I thought maybe you could help me color plan it. You have such a talent for bringing rugs together with the perfect choice of wool." Mari reached into the woven basket she gripped in her right hand and pulled out a pattern.

"My, this is interesting," I said, gazing at the images drawn on the linen background—dollar bills, a gavel, a rug hook. It didn't make sense to me.

"Yes, it's my tribute rug to Hilda," Mari said. "They represent her life—her love for hooking, when she worked at the bank, her time on the city council." She pointed to the various objects as she spoke.

"Oh, I see now," I said, nodding. Porkchop curled at my feet, clearly not interested in the rug.

"Mari, what a very nice gesture, but I've always been curious. You and Hilda had a strange relationship. I mean, she married your ex-husband, after all," I said.

Mari laughed. "She did me a favor. Why, I'd have handed the two-timing liar to her on a silver platter if I could."

Lucy, who stood next to me as Mari and I talked, gasped.

"Don't look so shocked, Lucy. I should have left Mac years before, only the boys needed me. It's difficult raising two boys on your own."

"What about child support? Wouldn't it have helped?" I asked, knowing nothing about the cost of raising children.

Mari shook her head. "He made peanuts in those days, fancied himself a great inventor."

"But I thought he'd successfully invented something to do with cars," Lucy said.

"True, but we'd already been married a long time. By then, the boys were attending high school," Mari said.

"I guess you get in a rut. It's easier to stay than move on. So how can I help you with your pattern?" Lucy asked, pointing to Mari's rug.

I walked over to Lucy's checkout counter. "Before you two get involved, let me pay for my wool so Porkchop and I can get out of your hair."

After I paid Lucy, my dog and I headed home, where work on an article for *Kid Science* magazine waited for me.

* * *

I stretched my arms over my head then glanced down at my buddy who was curled at my feet. "Porkchop, I don't know about you, but I'm starved." I'd been bent over my computer since arriving home from The Ewe. Why did I always wait until pushed up against a deadline to finish an article? I hit send and winged off my masterpiece on the life cycle of hummingbirds for a future issue of the magazine.

I shut down my laptop and stood. Porkie trotted next to me to check out what the refrigerator held to satisfy our hunger. The phone rang as I entered the kitchen. My caller ID said Lucy waited on the other end. "Hi Lucy. Thanks for your help this morning. I haven't picked up my hook since leaving you, but I hope to get to it this evening."

"Sam," Lucy sobbed, "Sergeant Peters is here with a search warrant."

CHAPTER TWENTY-TWO

"Lucy, calm down. Take a deep breath. Is Ralph there?" I asked, clutching my phone.

"No, he's at Dr. Plunkett's, getting a root canal," Lucy said, mentioning our local dentist.

I groaned silently to myself. Nothing against the doc, but I hate all dental visits. He could be the studliest guy in town, but hang me by my toes before I voluntarily visited him. Twice a year for a cleaning is more than enough time in the dental chair for me.

"I guess that puts him incommunicado," I said.

"Yes." Lucy sobbed into the phone. "This is Ralph's first appointment, and Doctor Plunklett said it would last about ninety minutes. Ralph won't be home for another hour. Oh, Sam, what am I to do? Sergeant Peters said he got a tip about something to do with Hilda's death. Saaaam," Lucy wailed. "Honestly, he says he's looking for a bracelet, but I don't know what kind. Help me, pleeease?"

"Peters, the knucklehead. Don't worry. He's on a wild-goose chase. I'll come right over." She would need a shoulder to lean on until Ralph returned from warming the dentist's chair. I had certainly leaned on hers enough when I was going through my divorce from George.

Lucy hiccupped. "Thank you, Sam. I didn't know who to call. I can always count on you for help."

I could hear Peters in the background as he barked orders to what I assumed were other officers at The Ewe. "And Lucy, don't say a word to Sergeant Peters until I get there," I warned. In Lucy's emotional condition, Joe would have her confessing to every murder this side of New York City.

I hung up with Lucy and glanced down at my dog curled up on the sofa next to me. "Porkchop, I'm sorry to disturb your nap, but Lucy needs us." I pushed off the sofa and walked over to the coat rack standing next to my front door and snatched his leash off a hook. As I pulled on my coat, I looked back at the tranquil setting. A now-cold cup of tea sat on the trunk in front of my sofa. My abandoned hooking was spread out on the cushions. I exhaled a sigh. Facing Joe Peters was never a treat on the best of days, but with him trying to accuse a good friend of murder, the scene at The Ewe didn't look promising. My hackles flared up, and I wasn't even out my front door.

Porkchop and I arrived at Lucy's shop about ten minutes later and spied two squad cars hugging the curb. The light bar flashed red and blue on top of one. Joe's car, I presumed. Leave it to him to announce his arrival to the whole neighborhood. Discreet is not his middle name. I wouldn't have put it past him to burst into the store with his gun drawn.

"Lucy," I called, pushing The Ewe's door open. I came to an abrupt halt. My eyes widened at the scene unfolding before me. Lucy's meticulously stacked wool, usually lining the walls of her store in cubbies, lay strewn all over the oak table in the middle of the room. Green wool mixed in with yellow, blue thrown on top of red.

Lucy ran out of her back room into my outstretched arms. "Sam, you're here," she sobbed. "Look what's become of all my lovely wool. I'll never make any sense of this mess. I might as well hang a for sale sign on the front door after Sergeant Peters finishes here." Tears streamed down her pale face. Her usually meticulously arranged white hair lay tangled about her head. Her once crisply ironed flowered shirt hung wrinkled and untucked from a pair of brown corduroy slacks. In other words, my neat-as-a-pin friend was a wreck.

"Now calm down. We'll make this all right after he and his men leave. You know the Loopy Ladies depend on you. We could never survive without you feeding our wool addictions. We'd go into withdrawal. You wouldn't want to deal with a bunch of wool-crazy women." I patted her on the back as she hiccupped sobs into my shoulder.

Lucy raised her head and gave me a faint smile. "Oh, Sam, I don't know what I'd do without you and the other ladies."

"What brought Peters here?"

I could hear Joe as he talked to his men in the back room.

Lucy grabbed a tissue from a box sitting next to the cash register on her checkout counter. She shrugged. "Something about a bracelet. I had been busy in the dye room stirring a pot of wool I brewed up. I need to get the right shade of blue for Mari's memory rug of Hilda that she mentioned earlier. The sound of sirens coming down the street caught my attention. They sounded awfully close, so curious, I came to the front room here to see if I could spot them. Next thing I know, Sergeant Peters banged on the door and said he held a search warrant for The Ewe."

"Did he mention a specific type of bracelet?" I asked. I looked around the room's mess. Judging by all the stacks of wool he and his men searched through, they sought something hidden in them. But people loved to rummage through Lucy's wool. Wouldn't she be foolish to hide anything in it that implicated herself in Hilda's murder? It wasn't like a missing gun or knife needed to be found. The police already held the murder weapon, a small pin dipped in arsenic.

"No, he instructed his men to start searching the stacks of wool. He must have told them beforehand what to search for." Lucy glanced around the room. "What am I going to do?" she sobbed.

I pulled out a chair from the wool-covered table and guided Lucy into it. "Now, sit here. Have you called Alan Rosenberg?"

"My lawyer? Do you think I should call him?" Lucy looked up at me with bewildered, red-rimmed eyes. She sat twisting her fingers together.

Nodding, I reached into my pocket for my cell phone. Lucy and I shared the same lawyer, so I scrolled my phone's contact list for his number. I didn't trust Joe Peters or his motives.

I punched the contact button for his number and waited for his secretary to answer. "Betty, this is Sam Davies," I said when she answered. I explained the situation at The Ewe and asked if Alan could come over.

I wrinkled my forehead at her answer. Alan had flown out of town this morning to a legal convention and wouldn't arrive home until tomorrow night. What to do now? I thanked

Betty and assured her she didn't need to disturb him. I could handle the situation. How, I didn't know. I disconnected then hit Hank's number. Maybe he'd know about Joe's mission. Drat, it went to his voice mail. "Hank, it's Sam. Can you give me a call when you get this message? I'm at Lucy's store. Joe Peters and some other officers have descended on her shop. He barged in waving a search warrant. The place looks like a tornado blew through. Lucy said they were searching for a bracelet."

A low growl drew my attention to the floor. Porkchop had sat so quietly at my feet while I dealt with Lucy, I'd forgotten he was here. I tightened my grip on his leash as the object of his displeasure walked into the room. Joe Peters. A plastic bag dangled from his hand. Two young officers followed behind him. Their crisply pressed uniforms hugged their youthful bodies. Were they recent graduates from the police academy? New recruits, perfect fodder for Joe to impress with his police skills.

"Mrs. Foster, do you recognize this?" he asked, holding the bag before Lucy for her inspection.

This time, I gasped. The bag contained a Hooker bracelet, like the one some of the Loopy Ladies wore. But more importantly, it looked to be Hilda's. These gems sparkled more under the store lights than our rhinestones. Could this be the one torn from Hilda's wrist at Lucy's hook-in? Was it the one someone had tried to pawn in Albany?

I glanced at Lucy. The blood drained from her face and her hands shook as she reached out for the bag. She opened her mouth to speak.

I stepped between her and Peters. "Lucy, don't say a thing. Not until you can get in touch with Alan Rosenberg."

Joe glared at me. If his eyes could have shot a laser beam at me, I'd crumple into a pile of cinders on the floor right now.

"Get on the phone and call your lawyer," Joe gritted out between clenched teeth. His tone of voice took on a hard edge. The veins in his neck bulged. Poor Joe not getting his own way didn't sit well with him, especially when he was trying to impress the young recruits.

I glanced over his shoulder and noticed the newbie cops starting to squirm. I'm guessing they didn't care for Joe badgering a woman old enough to be their grandmother. I didn't think intimidating senior citizens was a scenario practiced at the academy.

"Sandy, I mean Joe, her lawyer flew to a convention this morning and won't be home until tomorrow night. Can't your questions wait until he returns?" I asked.

He scowled at me, whether because I'd accidentally— well, maybe on purpose—called him by the nickname our kindergarten class christened him with after he peed in our sandbox or because he saw me as hindering his grilling of Lucy.

"How do I know she'll stick around until her lawyer returns?" he asked, resting his hand on his holster. Funny how you notice strange things when under stress. The buckle of his utility belt strained on its last hole. I figured the result of one too many doughnuts from the Doughnut Haven drive-thru.

I rolled my eyes. "For heaven's sake. Where do you think she's going to go? Make a run for the border? Get serious. I'll take full responsibility for Lucy. You'll have plenty of opportunity to question her after her lawyer returns."

I turned to Lucy, who had remained quiet during Joe's and my exchange. Did she have a crazed look in her eyes? She wouldn't be hiding something, would she? Like maybe she did murder Hilda? After all, people did kill because of money. Or what if Ralph murdered Hilda because of his brother's suicide? Nah, Lucy and Ralph couldn't commit murder, could they? What did Hank tell me? Nice people commit murder all the time. I swallowed hard and hoped I wouldn't regret my decision to make sure she showed up at the police station when Alan returned.

CHAPTER TWENTY-THREE

———

"Have you tried reaching Ralph? Shouldn't his root canal have ended by now?" I asked, glancing around the store at the mess left behind by Sergeant Peters and his rookies. Piles of wool once folded, sorted by color, and stacked in neat piles lay tumbled on the oak table, chairs, and the floor. I couldn't even imagine how overwhelmed Lucy must feel right now. The job of putting everything back in order would take hours, if not days.

"I've tried his cell a couple of times and left messages, but it always goes to his voice mail." Lucy smiled and continued, "He's not very good about carrying his phone with him. Usually, he leaves it in his car." She shook her head. A glimmer of fondness filled her blue eyes. She and Ralph lived a true love story. What some might think of as irritating, unable to get in touch with the hubby, she thought of as one of his endearing quirks. "The twenty-first century and phones have not caught up with Ralph."

"I completely understand. Have you ever noticed the number of people crossing streets with their eyes glued to their phones? It's amazing more fatalities haven't occurred," I said, reaching for a pile of wool and refolding it. I glanced at my watch. The black hands pointed to 4:30 p.m. "Candie has finished work now. I'll give her a call. She can come over and help put this place back in order. Do you want me to call any of the other Loopy Ladies to help? With all of us pitching in, we could have this place in order in no time." At least I hoped so.

Her hair swung about her shoulders as she shook her head emphatically. "Oh no, I don't want anyone else knowing what happened here today. I'm too embarrassed."

I walked over to Lucy and placed an arm around her shoulder. "Lucy, they'd want to help. They're here for you no matter what happens."

She lowered herself into one of the chairs surrounding the table. Porkchop walked over and stood on his hind legs and placed his head on her lap. His warm, chocolate-brown eyes stared up at her. My sweet dog always sensed when a person needed comforting. Lucy pulled a shredded tissue out of her sweater pocket and dabbed at the tears flowing down her cheeks. "I know, but I can't face them right now."

I patted Lucy on the shoulder. "Okay. I'll only call Candie, if it's all right with you. You know she wouldn't breathe a word about what happened here today."

Lucy nodded her head. "I know. Working for the mayor, she probably already knows about Peters' visit."

I flipped open my cell phone, and yes, Ralph isn't the only techno-challenged person. I punched in Candie's number.

Candie answered on the second ring. "Hey, cousin. You've caught me getting into Precious. What's up?"

Lucy was in good hands, or should I say paws, so I walked to the back dying room. I heard Lucy cooing and mumbling to Porkchop about what a good dog he was. Porkie lapped it up. His tail wagged like a child with the American flag on the fourth of July.

I kept my voice low so Lucy wouldn't have to relive the events of the day. I related to Candie what Peters and company had done to the shop and about their find.

She replied that Mark had told her of Peters' actions today. As mayor, I knew the police constantly updated him on the progress of the investigation into crimes like murder.

"Sugar, I'll arrive at The Ewe as soon as my dear Precious can wing me there," Candie said then hung up.

The bell over the door chimed. Walking back into the main room, I saw Ralph, who had entered the store. His mouth dropped open as he took in the scene of wool chaos.

Lucy sprang from her chair and ran into his arms. Between sobs, she relayed what had happened this afternoon and how Joe Peters discovered a Hooker bracelet tucked into a pile of wool in the dying room.

Ralph clutched Lucy to him with one arm and ran a hand that shook through his hair. That caused his wavy gray hair to stand on end like a rooster's comb.

"I know he thinks because he found the bracelet here in our store that one of us killed Hilda," Lucy sobbed.

Ralph held Lucy at arm's length and gazed into her watery eyes. "He's plain crazy. Why, a bunch of you ladies bought those bracelets when you went to a hook-in last year, right?"

Lucy sniffled then blew her nose. "Yes." She nodded. "They were a big hit at the show. I think they even sold out by the time the hook-in ended. You know how we all get a kick out of calling ourselves hookers."

Ralph smiled. "I love the reaction people give me when they ask if you still work. I reply, 'Yeah, she rakes in pretty good money as a hooker.'" He chuckled. "Makes for some pretty good conversation at Maxwell's Pub on dart night, too."

I heaved a sigh of relief as a faint smile twitched on Lucy's lips. The definition of true love stood before me, when your partner could make you smile even in the most devastating circumstances. And I'd say being a murder suspect rated as pretty devastating. I hoped Hank and I could come to their level of closeness someday, and sooner rather than later.

"Ralph's right, you know, Lucy. The bracelet Joe Peters took out of here could belong to anyone. They must have sold a gazillion of them at that hook-in. I mean, I bet every Loopy Lady has one. I know I do, and so does Candie," I said. Ralph looked from Lucy to me. I think he noticed for the first time that I was there.

Ralph scanned the shop. "We have some cleaning to do."

I laughed. "What an understatement. I called Candie. She should arrive soon to lend us a hand."

As if she had channeled my thoughts, Candie stood at The Ewe's front door. She juggled a large pizza box in her arms and shouted for me to let her in.

A barking Porkchop beat me to the door. I swear he has ESP. Somehow, he knew his favorite person, outside of me and possibly Hank, my dear cousin Candie, was bringing his favorite people food, pizza.

I didn't usually stray from his vet-prescribed dog food, but he played me for a sucker when we dined on pizza. He always managed to wrangle my crust out of me. Luckily, it didn't happen too often or we'd both be hitting the gym more than three times a week.

I yanked open The Ewe's door. Porkchop jumped at Candie's feet, trying to get to the box's contents.

"Porkie, behave yourself. You'll eat some crust soon enough," I said, trying to calm him.

Candie walked over to the checkout counter and placed the box down. She unbuttoned her red and black wool plaid coat and scanned the room. "Pheweee, you certainly didn't exaggerate the mess Sergeant Peters left behind. The very idea that he would think Lucy capable of doing any harm to a flea, let alone murdering someone, is preposterous. I'd love to string him up by his ba— I mean toes."

The three of us laughed. Leave it to Candie to lighten the mood.

I pointed to the pizza box. "Candie brought us some sustenance to help get us through the giant task before us. Lucy, do you have any paper plates around here?"

Lucy nodded. "I do. Back in the dye room. I keep them here for my lunch. In fact, I think I may have some soda in the refrigerator back there, too."

As Lucy scurried out of the room to fetch the paper plates, Ralph said, "Let's clear a space at the table so we can eat." He pointed to the checkout counter. "Put some of the wool over there."

Ralph, Candie, and I gathered armfuls of fabric and dumped them on the counter. Lucy's usually meticulously folded wool lay in a heap next to the pizza box.

Lucy returned to the room and handed us each a paper plate. We selected a slice of pepperoni pizza then settled at the table.

"Well, it's obvious to me someone planted the bracelet there," Candie said, dabbing her mouth with a napkin Lucy supplied.

"Planted it?" Ralph, Lucy, and I asked at the same time. My cousin, who in her spare time wrote romance novels, owned a very vivid imagination. But it usually leaned towards unbridled love and loud sighs of passion.

"Don't y'all see? Why, it's as plain as Porkie loving pizza crust." Porkchop's ears perked up at the mention of his name. "Someone wants to blame Lucy and Ralph for Hilda's murder."

Lucy stopped chewing and placed her half-eaten piece of pizza on her plate. "Who would hate us so much to pin her murder on us?"

Ralph shook his head in disbelief. "Darned if I know."

I caught on to what my cousin said. "I don't think it's a matter of hate so much as an act of desperation. They want to deflect any suspicion away from them and onto you."

"Right," Candie said. She reached under the table and handed Porkchop the crust of her pizza.

"Lucy, who has been in to shop since Hilda's murder?" I hoped to narrow the field of possible suspects. Whoever planted the bracelet in a stack of wool must be the murderer.

Lucy stared up at the ceiling as if she tried to recollect who might have stopped in The Ewe. "You know, it's funny, but since Saturday, I've worked nonstop. I think every Loopy Lady, plus a few others, came into the store, even Mari Adams. They all wanted to gossip about Hilda's death."

Great! I thought. *She certainly narrowed the field of murder suspects.*

CHAPTER TWENTY-FOUR

———

Candie dabbed at her lips with a napkin. "Oh my, I couldn't stuff another pepperoni in me if I tried."

I smiled to myself. My cousin, raised by our manners-perfect memaw, never swiped a napkin across her lips. No, she gently dabbed away any offending crumbs.

Candie glanced around the studio. "Lordy, Lucy, it will take us a month of Sundays to get this place in order. It's more than the four of us can tackle. We need to call in reinforcements."

I nodded in agreement. "I told her we should rally the Loopy Ladies." I reached down and gave Porkchop a final piece of pizza crust. Bad move on my part, but it is the only thing I've ever served him from the table.

Lucy, busy clearing the dirty paper plates, cups, and napkins from the table, looked up. "Yes, they are all my dear friends, but I don't know if I could face anyone right now." She glanced at Ralph. Tears filled her eyes.

He squeezed her hand. "They're right, sweetie." He spread out his hand and motioned to the wool-scattered room. "We need help. It will take us hours to clean up this mess."

Lucy heaved a deep sigh. "All right, call the ladies and find out who can come over and help. It's late, though, dinnertime."

"Great. We have twelve Loopy Ladies, including you, Lucy. With Ralph that will make thirteen. If everyone can come, we'll have this place in order in no time. Do you have a list of their phone numbers?" I pulled my cell phone out of my jeans' pocket.

Lucy nodded. Ralph finished gathering up our dinner mess while she walked over to the checkout counter. She opened a drawer and retrieved a piece of paper then handed it to me. Written on it was a list of names and phone numbers for the Loopy Ladies, plus a few of her clients.

I showed Candie the names. "You take the first half, and I'll call the second. We'll get through the list faster."

* * *

Fifteen minutes later, I snapped my phone closed. Candie glanced up from her bejeweled phone.

"Well, I contacted everyone on my half of the list except for Jane Burrows. Her momma said she needed to go to an emergency meeting at the library," Candie said.

"What kind of emergency could the library have? Especially in the children's department. Did someone leave a lollipop in one of the books?" I asked, chuckling.

Ralph cleared his throat. "The reason it took me so long to get home from the dentist this afternoon is because I stopped off at Clyde's barber shop. I needed a trim." He ran a hand along the back of his neck. "You know his shop holds forth as gossip central for Wings Falls." We all nodded. "Well, anyway, Clyde said a client mentioned that the library's budget came up short this quarter."

I frowned. "Came up short? What do you mean 'came up short'?"

"It's audit time for the library's financial books, and money is missing," he said as he walked towards the dye room with our dinner trash.

I looked at Candie. Was she thinking what I was? Could Jane Burrows have murdered Hilda for her bracelet? She could probably guess at the value of the bracelet. Maybe she tried to pawn it to replace the missing library monies.

"Did you contact everyone on your half of the list?" Candie tucked her phone into her purse.

I shook my head. "No, Roberta Holden's husband answered the phone. He said she was sick and took to her bed. But didn't you say she came to the store earlier, Lucy?"

"Yes, and she looked fine to me. Maybe she ate something, and it didn't agree with her?"

Or maybe something didn't agree with her coming to The Ewe tonight, I thought.

I looked up from my phone. "You have Mari's number on this list, too. I think I'll give her a call. Maybe joining with fellow hookers might brighten her spirits. What do you think?"

Lucy, Ralph, and Candie nodded in agreement.

Lucy paused from folding a piece of wool. "Before the police arrived, I had finished dying the wool she wanted for her memory rug of Hilda. I think I'll give it to her as a present. You know, let bygones be bygones. To show I bear no ill will towards Hilda."

Ralph drew his wife into a hug and placed a kiss on the top of her snow-white hair. "You are a very kind person," he said.

Watching the loving couple made me smile. With hearts so full of love and generosity as theirs, who could picture either of them as Hilda's killer?

I ran my finger down the list until I reached Mari's phone number then punched it into my cell phone. It rang five times before a young man answered. Her son, I presumed. "Hi. Are you one of Mari's sons?"

"Yes, I'm Jason. Who wants to know?"

I knew she had shared two sons with her ex, Jason and Tommie. I had only met them a few times when they were younger. I don't think I'd recognize them now if I fell over them. They were grown and in their twenties.

I asked Jason if his mom was in, but he said she was called out of town suddenly. A sick uncle or something. She'd be home tomorrow.

"Okay, I hope everything is fine with her uncle." I flipped my phone shut and stood staring at it.

"What's wrong, Sam? Did someone ask you to explain the theory of relativity?" Candie asked.

"Huh," I said, shaking my head trying to wrap my brain around Jason's answer.

"What did Mari say to make you look so confused?" Candie clarified.

"She's not home. Her son, Jason, said she'd left town. Something about a sick uncle. He didn't say much more." I shoved my cell phone into my jeans back pocket.

"Wow. Something must have happened after she left this morning," Lucy said. She picked up another piece of wool and refolded it. "The poor woman. First her best friend Hilda, and now something's wrong with her uncle. I hope all goes well."

The bell over the shop's door chimed. We all turned as Patsy Ikeda entered with her dog, Hana, a beautiful Japanese Spitz.

Porkchop's tail began to wag. He and Hana became best buds after Patsy started bringing Hana with her for our Monday morning Loopy Lady gathering. Porkchop, already a Monday morning regular, readily bonded with the cute white ball of fur. Too bad I prided myself as a dutiful dog parent and had made sure he was spayed and that Hana wasn't a she. They might have produced some interesting offspring. I imagined sausage-shaped white cotton candy with four legs, prancing around The Ewe.

"Hi, Patsy," I greeted her. "I'm glad you brought Hana. He can keep Porkchop company while we try to put the shop back in order."

"We do have a big job ahead of us." She turned in a circle and eyed the wool chaos. Patsy bent and unleashed Hana, much to Porkchop's delight. The two dogs jumped and tumbled in greeting.

Within minutes of Patsy's arrival, the remaining Loopy Ladies arrived. Susan Mayfield brought two apple pies from her restaurant, Momma Mia's. She said their produce supplier gave Brian a deal on apples that he couldn't refuse. As a result, Brian spent the afternoon elbow-deep in flour, turning out the pies.

Who were we to refuse such a fantastic offer? The pizza I ate would wear off soon enough, and apple pie was certainly a pick-me-up to look forward to.

Helen Garber, in her usual take-charge manner, had everyone organized in no time at all. She assigned us all a color to be responsible for refolding and stacking on the shelves and in the cubbies. She designated Candie and me the blue team. Susan and Cookie Harrington were to refold any whites and creams they found. Patsy and Marybeth Higgins drew the red lot. Anita Plum and Gladys O'Malley had the greens to neaten-up. Ralph and Lucy were assigned all the blacks and browns, and Helen gave herself the job of corralling the oranges and yellow. It figured, as those colors dominated her wardrobe choices.

My lips curved into a smile as I observed this very diverse group of ladies and one gentleman all working together to help their dear friends, Lucy and Ralph, restore some order back into their lives. But such was the beauty of this group of ladies. We may have differing personalities—Helen Garber had her brash and outspoken ways. Marybeth Higgins was as quiet as the proverbial church mouse. The ages ranged from our youngest, Cookie Harrington, who I guessed to be in her late twenties, to the oldest, Gladys O'Malley, who sometimes admitted to hovering in her early eighties. Gladys held up a Kelly-green piece of wool to her hair and asked Anita if it matched her hair color. Since this was March, Gladys had dyed her hair in honor of the upcoming Saint Patrick's Day celebration. Yes, my chest puffed up with pride when I included myself as a member of the Loopy Ladies.

Helen glanced up from a stack of orange wool. "So, what happened to Roberta and Jane tonight?"

I explained about Roberta not feeling well and Jane's emergency audit meeting.

"Humph," she replied. "Jane wouldn't take a penny from the library. It's her life. I imagine she will leave what little money she does have to the library when she passes away."

Everyone gathered around the table agreed. I silently prayed she was right. Despite her odd ways, Jane was a good and honest person. Who was I to say a woman in her late fifties, living with her mother, was a little strange? Heck, I lived in my childhood home with Donny Osmond staring down at me every night when I climbed into bed.

"Did you say Roberta felt sick?" Susan asked, her arms full of a stack of white wool.

"Yes, I called her, but her husband said she took to her bed. She was feeling poorly," I said, admiring a piece of blue wool that I had folded. Should I put the wool aside and buy it or not?

"How odd. You know I have to pass their house on the way here, and I saw Roberta and her husband walking to their car," Susan said.

"Maybe he was driving her to one of those Doc-in-a-Box clinics that have sprung up recently," Lucy said, handing Ralph a stack of wool to place in a cubby.

"She looked pretty dressed up to be going to visit a doctor—heels, a fancy coat and hat," Susan said.

What? According to my conversation with him, she was too sick to take my phone call.

"Sam called Mari to ask if she would like to join us. You know, we could make her a part of the group since she lost Hilda," Candie added, placing a royal blue piece of wool next to her handbag. I bet it was going home with her.

A chorus of "so sweet" and "how kind" circled the table.

"Yes, but her son Jason said she was called out of town. Something about a sick uncle needing her attention." I put the piece of wool I'd been admiring aside to purchase later. At this rate, more wool would be coming home with me than I refolded.

"What uncle?" Helen asked. Her piercing blue eyes nailed me with her question. I would have hated to have been one of her history students who forgot an assigned report, back when she taught high school.

Her laser-like gaze made me squirm in my seat, and I hadn't even done anything. "I don't know. Jason didn't elaborate."

"Well, he must have been mistaken. All her uncles have passed away. She has a couple of aunts still living, but no uncles. I taught that boy. He never could get anything right."

No living uncles? Surely, Jason would know if a relative was dead or alive.

CHAPTER TWENTY-FIVE

————

I flopped back into my chair. My eyes traveled around Lucy's shop. Who knew folding wool could be so exhausting. The rest of the Loopy Ladies were as tired as me, if the way their shoulders drooped and the lull in the spirited conversations indicated anything. I reached down to scratch Porkie's head. He had behaved perfectly while we were busy putting the shop back in order. He sat at my feet and chewed on a rawhide bone. Ralph gave Porkchop the bone after he'd eaten our pizza crusts.

"Oops." I had accidentally knocked over a large canvas bag Candie had placed between us. "Sorry, cuz." I scooped up the contents that had spilled onto the floor. I didn't want Porkchop or me to step on them.

My fingers wrapped around a pamphlet. I picked it up and noticed it was a campaign flyer for Mayor Mark's reelection.

"Geez, is it that time of year again? Time to get out and hit the campaign trail, so to speak, in Wings Falls?" I flipped through the flyer. A picture of Mark, with his shirt sleeves rolled up and talking to a group of senior citizens, graced the front.

Candie nodded, auburn curls bouncing against her smooth white cheeks. "Yes, before you know it election time will be here. Mark doesn't take one vote for granted."

In my humble opinion, our mayor was the best thing to happen to Wings Falls in years. I didn't only feel this way because he was a friend and also dated Candie. Mark ranked up there as a good man and was honest as they come. Before he was elected to mayor four years ago, corruption ran rampant in my small town. Too many people had stuck their fingers into the treasury pot. During his term as mayor, he had cleaned up the city. Sometimes he ruffled a few feathers, but he had put the city treasury back in the black and led the way in championing for our senior citizens. He made sure the schools got the funds they need, helped businesses thrive, and took care of our homeless and low-income families.

"Is anyone thinking of challenging him?" I couldn't imagine a single person who stood a chance against Mark and his record of accomplishments.

Candie leaned close to me. "Rumors say Bret Hargrove may challenge him. You can understand why it is important we put these flyers out sooner than later."

"You mean the owner of the audio store on Main Street, The Sound Machine?"

Candie's brow creased. "Yes, him. He's made noises about how he can run Wings Falls much better than Mark. He wants to turn it into a tourist destination to rival Lake George."

I rolled my eyes. Lake George was a lovely lakeside town about fifteen minutes from Wings Falls, but I didn't think we needed the hordes of tourists who descended there every year from May to September or the disruption to our quiet town that they brought. My town hadn't earned the name Hometown USA by a major magazine years ago for nothing. We loved the quaint, homey atmosphere of Wings Falls.

"Candie, did you say you have some flyers for Mark's reelection?" Susan Mayfield had piped up. "Give me a bunch. We'll put them in the restaurant." Susan laughed. "Maybe I'll place a couple on each table for the customers to read while waiting for their meals. They would certainly make for good dinner conversation."

The rest of the Loopy Ladies joined in the laughter.

Cookie Harrington had held out her slim brown hand to Candie. "Hand me some, too. I'll place them on the checkout counter at the vet's. Speaking of which, I'd better get going. I have the late shift tonight." Cookie not only worked as the receptionist at Wings Falls Animal Hospital, but sometimes she pulled duty as a night attendant for the animals boarding overnight.

"Thanks so much." Candie handed a stack of flyers to both Susan and Cookie. "It might be a tough race this time around. Mark has no idea what kind of campaign Bret will run.

A lot of new people have moved into the area. They aren't aware of all he has accomplished for the town."

Lucy stood and tucked a strand of white hair behind an ear. "Well, he has Ralph's and my votes. He certainly helped us out when the sidewalk in front of the store needed replacing."

Helen nodded her head. "I remember when it was a cracked mess."

"It was an accident waiting to happen," Lucy said. "But Mark got a crew here to fix it not long after he was elected."

I glanced up from the brochure. "Our Mark. A man of action." I turned to Candie. "Oh, that could be his campaign slogan—Mark Hogan, a man of action."

Candie bounced in her chair and clapped her hands. "I love it. I'll mention it to him."

"Everything is back in order," I said, eyeing the shelves all restocked with bundles of wool. Any trace of Joe Peters and company having descended on The Ewe was gone. "Porkchop and I better get home. He needs a proper meal of his kibble. A day of eating pizza scraps doesn't bode well for his waistline."

The ladies and Ralph laughed as I clipped Porkchop's leash to his collar. I grabbed the wool I had set aside for my stash and walked over to the counter to pay Lucy. I pulled out my wallet, but she pushed my hand away.

"I can never repay you for what you did for Ralph and me today. Please take the wool as a sign of my love and gratitude for you."

Heat crawled up my neck. I reached out and folded Lucy in my arms. "Lucy, you're like a sister to all of us. Of course, we're here for you and Ralph." Tears brimmed in Lucy's eyes as she whispered a simple thank you in my ear.

I patted Lucy on the back then tugged Porkchop towards me. "Come on, Porkie, time to go home and get some kibble." At the mention of kibble, his tail wagged. The day's events must have exhausted him as much as me. After waving goodbye to everyone, we headed home.

* * *

"Okay, Porkie, it's back to your plain ol' kibble. No more pizza crusts. You have to stay in shape for our book

signings once *Porkchop, the Wonder Dog* hits the bookstores."
He sat at my feet with his head cocked to one side.

Once inside my cozy home, I'd changed into my
pajamas—a pair of well-worn black and red plaid flannel
bottoms and a black fleece top with a smiling moose head
embroidered on it. They were a Christmas present a few years
back from my parents. They may have retired to sunny Florida,
but they hadn't forgotten the cold upstate New York winters.

My doorbell buzzed. Porkchop barked and ran towards
the front door. The schoolhouse clock hanging on the wall next
to my fireplace read eight o'clock. "Who could it be this time of
night?" I asked my empty living room as I walked to the front
door.

I peeked out the window next to the door and spied a
very weary Hank leaning against the iron railing on the steps
leading up to my door. Without the metal support of the railing,
he probably would have collapsed.

I opened the door. My heart leapt into my throat as
Hank pushed away from the railing. His baby blue eyes
searched my face. I spread my arms wide. He walked right into
the unspoken warmth I offered him. Even Porkchop could sense
Hank's tiredness. Instead of his usual jumping at Hank for pats
and scratchies behind the ears, he padded next to us towards the
living room sofa.

I shoved aside the bundles of wool Lucy gave me
earlier at The Ewe, now spread out on the sofa. Hank sank onto
the sofa with a sigh. Porkchop jumped up and curled onto his
lap.

"Porkie, come on sweetie. Hank's tired." My dog stared
up at me with his liquid brown eyes as I nudged him onto the
floor.

Hank reached down and gave Porkchop the scratchies
he wanted. "I'm okay, Sam. It's been a long day. Dealing with
Peters in this investigation is no picnic."

"No, Porkie needed to go out anyway. Give me a
minute. I'll be right back." Porkchop's ears perked up at the
words "go out." I guess I said the right words because he
scampered towards the kitchen.

My dad had built a white picket fence around our
backyard when I was a child to keep me from wandering off.

Now I welcomed the idea of opening the kitchen door to let Porkchop out to do his business. I didn't have to accompany him, especially during this nasty cold March weather we still enjoyed.

"Come on, Porkie. Give a bark when you want to come back in," I said, giving his back end a nudge out the door. He ranked winter right up there where I did, right below having a head cold.

On my way back to the living room, I stopped at the refrigerator and snatched a cold beer for Hank.

He sat slumped against the back of the sofa, his lips parted. He snored softly. I placed the cold beer on the table next to him and reached for the blanket draped across the back.

"What? Oh, sorry, Sam. Guess I dozed off. Where's my buddy?" Hank asked, sitting up.

I laughed. "Outside, doing his thing. He was disappointed, though, that you didn't give him your undivided attention when you came in. There's a beer next to you if you want it," I said, nodding towards the bottle.

"Thanks. A Trails Head. It's been a long day. This will hit the spot." He reached for the beer and twisted off its cap.

I sat, mesmerized. My pulse ratcheted up. His long, slim fingers wrapped around the bottle. He leaned his head back and took deep swallows of the amber liquid. I longed to pull him into my arms and soothe away his day's tiredness.

He placed the beer back onto the table and said, "Peters put a rush job on the bracelet his guys found today at The Ewe."

"What did they find? Is he going to arrest Lucy? I don't care what those lab guys find. Ralph and Lucy are innocent." I pounded the sofa cushion with my fists and babbled but I couldn't help myself. "So, what did they find?" I asked again, curling my legs up under me on the sofa.

Hank laughed. "Do you really want to know?"

I swatted his arm with a piece of wool lying next to me. "Hank, please can you tell me? I promise I won't tell a soul."

"It's no secret. The bracelet is paste," he said, grinning at my frustration.

"What?" I asked, frowning.

"Paste, as in fake. Not Hilda's," he said, drawing me into his arms.

"Why would anyone go to the trouble of planting a fake bracelet in Lucy's store? I mean, a bunch of us have the fake Hooker bracelets. Hilda owned the only real one. She always needed to one up everyone." I snuggled closer to Hank.

"I know. It doesn't make any sense, unless the killer wanted to throw us off track and buy themself more time," Hank said. He tipped my face up and gave me a long, sweet kiss.

"Umm, before we continue, I'd better let Porkchop in. I'm surprised he hasn't scratched at the door. In this cold weather, he's not usually out this long." I pushed myself off the sofa and headed towards the kitchen.

I flicked on the outside light, opened the kitchen door, and called out for Porkchop. My eyes searched the backyard for my little bundle of fur. My heart leapt into my throat. "Porkchop!" I screamed and tore down the back steps.

Kneeling in the soft snow, I cradled a limp Porkchop in my arms as tears streamed down my face.

CHAPTER TWENTY-SIX

———

Hank knelt beside me in the cold snow. He placed a hand on my shoulder. "Sam, he's breathing. We need to get him to Doc's right away."

Porkchop's small, limp body lay cradled in my arms. He pulled in shallow, labored breaths.

Dazed, I turned and stared up at Hank. "Huh," I said, barely focusing on his face. Tears clouded my vision.

"Here, hand me Porkchop. Get your coat and meet me at my car. I'll drive you to the vet's." Hank held his arms out to me.

I bent and kissed the top of Porkchop's head then passed him over to Hank. After I placed my precious pup safely in Hank's arms, I ran into the house and grabbed my poufy coat and purse. I shook off my snow-soaked slippers and slid my bare feet into the pair of rubber-bottom boots that sat by the front door. With no time to change out of my PJs, I tore open the front door and raced down my now, with the evening drop in temperature, ice-covered steps. It's a miracle I didn't wind up in the ER alongside Porkchop.

Hank sped out of the driveway and pointed his Jeep towards the animal hospital. Porkchop lay nestled in a pile of blankets on the car's back seat. Shallow breaths whispered from his mouth as if he was in a deep sleep. I snatched my cell phone from the dark depths of my purse and hit the speed dial button for the hospital. I sent prayers heavenward to Saint Francis, the patron saint of animals, to watch over my dog.

Cookie Harrington answered the phone on the second ring.

"Cookie! Oh, thank God, you answered," I choked out between sobs.

"Sam, is that you? I recognized your caller ID. Yes, today is our late night, but we're just about to close. What's the matter?" Cookie asked.

"It's Porkie. Something is terribly wrong with him. I'm on my way." I gazed back at my poor puppy and silently prayed he'd hang in until we arrived at the vet's.

"Drive carefully, Sam. Doc is here checking on a few of his patients. I'll have him meet you at the door," Cookie said in a voice meant to calm me down, but I don't think anything would do the trick right now outside of a fifth of whiskey.

"Thanks, Cookie. Hank will have us there in five minutes." I snapped my cell phone shut and hung on to my seat. At the speed Hank drove, I revised our arrival time down to two minutes.

Hank pulled into Wings Falls Animal Hospital and skidded his Jeep to a halt next to the entrance. The hospital's glass doors swung open. Doc Sorenson, his white lab coat flapping around his legs, raced out with a vet tech on his heels. I jumped out of the car and flung the back seat door open. The tech reached in and gingerly unwrapped Porkchop from his nest of blankets. My sweet Porkie didn't respond as the tech lifted him out. He lay in the tech's arms, snoring softly as if in a deep sleep.

"Ben, get blood tests started right away," Doc shouted over his shoulder.

Ben nodded and nudged the hospital's door open with his hip, careful not to disturb the precious bundle in his arms.

Hank climbed out of the car and stood at my side, his arm draped across my shoulder. Doc peppered us with questions as we followed him inside.

"Had Porkchop eaten anything unusual? When did he last eat or drink? How had he acted earlier today?"

My head spun with all the questions.

"Doc, I found this on the ground next to Porkchop." Hank held up a plastic bag containing a rawhide bone. I blinked. Why did I not find it unusual he'd have an evidence bag stuffed in his pocket? Then again, as a detective, he'd need them when investigating a crime.

My mouth fell open. "It resembles the bone Ralph gave Porkie earlier today at The Ewe."

"Are you certain, Sam?" Hank asked.

I fingered the bag. "Well, I didn't bring the bone home with me." I peered closer at the bag. "And this one has something smeared on it."

Doc held out his hand. "Here, give it to me. If I'm not mistaken, it looks like peanut butter. I need my lab to test it right away." He turned and hurried through the doors separating the reception area from the exam rooms and lab.

I sank onto one of the wooden benches that lined the wall of the reception room. Hank sat next to me and pulled me into the warmth of his body. A sob shuddered through me.

"Sam, he'll be fine. Doc will take good care of Porkchop. Before you know it, he'll jump up and down and beg for his treats."

I looked up at Hank. Tears flowed down my cheeks. "Are you sure, Hank?" My spine stiffened. I balled my hand into a fist and scrubbed away the tears. Anger now flowed through me. "Why would anyone want to harm my sweet puppy?"

"Sam, we don't know that for sure," Hank said, tucking a stray curl behind my ear.

Frustrated, I lashed out. "Come on, Hank! Why else would someone smear peanut butter on the bone if not to make Porkie eat something to harm him? It's an old trick. I do it all the time when he needs to take medicine. I bury it in a glob of peanut butter. He laps it up."

I straightened and stared at Hank. "Someone wants to get to me through Porkchop."

Nodding, he said, "Why do you think I became so upset when I learned you and Candie traveled into Albany and nosed around those pawn shops? Someone doesn't want you digging into Hilda's murder."

I clenched my fists at my side. "If they think I'm going to let this attack on Porkchop go, they have another think coming."

Hank pulled me close to him. "Sam, please let me take care of this. I don't want anything to happen to you. Or Porkchop. It's my job, you know, to solve crimes, and if I do say so myself, I'm pretty good at it."

I nodded but crossed my fingers. If this unknown person only meant harm to me, it would have been one thing, but since they'd now involved my Porkchop, they'd raised the stakes, and I wasn't about to let this go.

My body twitched with nervous energy. I needed to do something, anything. Waiting to talk to Doc was killing me. I felt like screaming, but instead I stood and paced the small reception area. I glanced at my watch and heaved a sigh. An hour had passed since we'd arrived at the vet's. When would Doc come out and tell us how Porkchop was doing?

The door to the exam room area opened, and Cookie stuck her head out. "Doc wants to see you." She motioned for us to follow her.

Finally!

Hank stood and reached for my hand. He gave it a gentle squeeze. "Sam, everything will be fine. Doc's the best there is."

I glanced up and gave him a weak smile, praying he was right.

Cookie led us down a narrow hall into a small room. A stainless-steel exam table occupied the middle of the room. A small counter lined one wall, and two metal chairs stood against another wall. Framed photographs of happy pet owners and their pets decorated the walls. Porkchop's and mine hung amongst them.

I'd no more sat down when Doc walked into the room. I leapt off my chair and crossed over to him. My tears started again as I asked, "How is my dog?"

Doc placed a hand in the pocket of his lab coat and drew out a piece of paper. Adjusting the wire-rimmed glasses sliding down his nose, he said, "Apparently, someone laced the peanut butter with a pretty strong dose of diphenhydramine."

Hank frowned. "What is that, Doc?"

The puzzled expression on my face must have told the doctor I was as clueless as Hank.

"The common name is Benadryl. You can purchase it over the counter at any drugstore. The most usual side effect is drowsiness. But more extreme cases can result in rapid heartbeat, breathing difficulties. Luckily, the amount Porkchop ingested only made him extremely tired."

Dazed, I sank unto my chair. "Why, *why* would anyone do such a thing?"

Hank reached for my hand. "I'll find out, Sam. I promise. Please, don't worry."

I looked up at Doc with a pleading look in my eyes. "Will he be all right? Can I take him home?"

"He'll be fine. He needs to sleep off the medicine. Dogs are pretty tough characters. Why, the other day a little guy came in here who ate some rat poison. Fortunately, his owner got him here in time for us to pump his stomach. A few hours later, the pup barked up a storm. I want to keep Porkchop overnight for observation. I'm sure you can take him home tomorrow."

"Can I visit with him before we leave?" I asked. I needed to pet his little furry body before I went home.

"Sure," Doc said.

He led us into the inner sanctum of the hospital, passing a room full of microscopes and shelves lined with jars full of what I presumed were medicines. Two more rooms were fitted out as operating rooms. Finally, we came to an area filled with pet cages. They varied from large to small, depending on the size of the occupant. We followed Doc to the end of a row of ten cages. Curled in a ball in the last cage slept my baby. I lifted the latch to the cage, reached in, and stroked his back. He stirred under my hand, nuzzling it with his nose. I bent, placed a kiss on his nose, and whispered, "I love you," to my dozing pet. I glanced up at Hank. "I think he knows I'm here." Tears threatened to start again.

Hank nodded. "I'm sure he does."

* * *

Assured Porkchop would be all right. I told Cookie on the way out I'd be back in the morning to pick him up. Hank and I then headed back to my house. He saw me inside then kissed me good night. We both knew I wouldn't be good company after tonight's events.

Alone, I went into my den and retrieved a pen and pad of paper from the scarred maple desk my dad had used. I sat and jotted down my list of suspects for Hilda's murder, but now as much as I hated to, I moved one to the top of the list and placed a star next to it—Ralph, who knew of Porkchop's love for rawhide bones.

CHAPTER TWENTY-SEVEN

"Oh, you poor darling. Dixie threw a conniption when I told her about that nasty person drugging you, whoever they are." Candie doted on her calico cat, Dixie, as much as I did Porkchop. "She wouldn't even play with her catnip mouse, and you know how she loves her catnip, as much as you love chewing on a rawhide bone."

My dear cousin sat next to me on my sofa and stroked Porkchop's head. She'd hurried over to my house on her lunch break. I had called her first thing this morning to tell her about what happened to Porkchop last night, but not before I had phoned the vet's as soon as they opened to check on Porkie. Thankfully, Connie was finishing up her night shift and answered my call. She connected me right away with Doc Sorenson, who reassured me that Porkchop had rested peacefully last night and could go home this morning. Not wasting any time, I threw on my coat and hurried over to collect my precious pup. When the vet assistant brought him out to the waiting room, you'd never guess we had all suffered through such a trying night. His tail wagged like crazy as soon as he saw me, and his sometimes-annoying barks sounded like music to my ears. Now he lay on my sofa, basking in his Aunt Candie's attention.

I laughed and shook my head. "Dixie feeling sorry for Porkchop? That would rank as a first."

"So, someone gave Porkchop a dose of Benadryl mixed in with peanut butter? Ewwww, how evil." Candie wrinkled her freckled nose.

"Those were the findings from Doc's lab. Hank thinks this might all tie into Hilda's death." The thought of someone trying to keep me from asking questions about Hilda's death by injuring my dog sent chills through me. I tightened my hands around my warm mug of tea.

Candie's mouth dropped open. Her Passion Pink lips formed an O. "Hank believes someone tried to silence you by hurting poor Porkie Workie?" she cooed, rubbing his stomach.

I rolled my eyes and nodded. "Yes, and he's warned me not to get involved any further."

Candie's head snapped up. "He's warned you not to get involved? That Yankee doesn't know us Parkers very well, does he? We don't take kindly to one of our own being hurt in any way, whether of the human or animal variety. Right, Porkchop?"

My dog raised his head, thumped the sofa cushion with his tail, and barked. Apparently, he fully agreed with her.

I placed my mug on the end table next to me. "This makes the second time someone tried to warn me off. Guess the murderer doesn't think I took my slashed tires seriously enough. Now he or she is hitting a little closer to home. I certainly don't want to put Porkchop in any more danger, but now they have gotten too personal for me to ignore."

"Right," Candie said with a vigorous shake of her head. "What's our plan of action to flush out this dirty scoundrel? I'd love to give them a dose of their own medicine. Maybe serve them a big ol' spoonful of peanut butter laced with Benadryl."

My mouth dropped open. Who knew my prim and proper Southern cousin could act so vengeful?

"Not us. Me." I took a sip of my tea, trying to hold back a laugh.

Candie's back stiffened. "Samantha Davies, if you plan to shut me out of any sleuthing, you can forget that crazy idea."

Tears flooded my eyes. "I love you, sweet cousin, but I couldn't live with myself if this person hurt you in any way because of my snooping."

"Honey, now wash that silly thought right out of your brain. Remember those summers you spent with me on Memaw Parker's farm?"

I nodded and swiped tears away. Fond memories flooded over me of the carefree days of our childhood when we played in our grandparents' fields.

"And remember all the scrapes we got into and out of?"

I nodded again.

"Well, I sure do hope you don't think I'm going to let you have all the fun and do this investigating on your own. We're a team. The Sleuthing Cousins."

The tears flowed down my cheeks again as I leaned over and gathered Candie in my arms for a hug. "Okay, you win. Like the old days, we're in this together."

"Bark!" Came from my dog.

"Oops," I laughed. Porkchop wiggled his long body out from between us. "Sorry, buddy. I didn't mean to catch you up in our hug."

"So where do you want to start?" Candie rubbed her hands together. "I guess we already have started, though, when we hit those pawn shops in Albany."

I smiled at my cousin's eagerness to help solve Hilda's murder. "Yes, I could excuse my slashed tires as a possible teen vandal, but drugging Porkchop becomes personal and aimed right at me."

"Someone is sending you a message, for sure," Candie said.

I slapped the sofa cushion. "Their message came in loud and clear, and I plan to send my own don't-mess-with-me message to the culprit."

"Way to go, girl." Candie high-fived me. "What now?"

"Ralph." I hated to say it, but he was a top possibility on my list of suspects.

"Ralph? Do you think he killed Hilda? You know he loves Porkchop. Whenever we stop at The Ewe, he hands him a treat or a rawhide bone." Candie's violet eyes widened. A look of understanding spread across her face.

"'You're right. He knows about Porkchop's love of those bones. He does have a motive. Remember, his brother loved Hilda and he committed suicide after she broke up with him. Then there's the business of her stealing Lucy's designs," I said. Ralph as the murderer became more and more possible to me.

"Right," Candie said. "Love and money can make a person do strange things." She glanced at her watch. "My lunch break ends soon. I'll meet you after work and we can go grill Ralph."

I laughed. "I think we'll have to be a little more subtle. Lucy stays open late tonight, so we'll drive over and try to discover what we can about Ralph's activities last night. I want to spend the day cuddling with Porkie." At the sound of his name, he raised his chocolate-brown eyes to me.

I walked my cousin to the door then returned to the sofa. I wanted to spend the afternoon snuggling with my dear Porkchop and try to figure out who wanted to harm him and, oh yes, kill Hilda. Hank might not want me meddling, but I wasn't about to let this attack on my pup be shoved under the so-called rug. The person who harmed Porkchop needed to pay for what they did.

* * *

As she had promised, Candie stopped by after work. "You ready to go sleuthing?" she asked as we stood on my porch.

I locked my front door. "Yes, the sooner we solve Hilda's murder, the safer Porkchop and I will feel."

"Hi, ladies. Going out?"

I looked up and waved. My next-door neighbor, Gladys, was tugging a trash can up her driveway.

Gladys's green curls peaked out of the wool cap pulled over her ears. "The air sure is a little nippy, but then, this is March. One never knows what to wear. Winter could have a grip on us one day, and the next, spring would be knocking at our door."

"The temperature certainly has dropped. We're on our way to Lucy's studio. I need more wool for my rug," I replied, tucking my mittened hands into the pockets of my coat. March did hold a myriad of weather surprises.

"Have fun. Got to get back inside to my Pookie Bear," Gladys said, referring to her live-in boyfriend, Frank Gilbert. She pointed to the trash can. "This is his job, but gout's laid him low."

I waved and walked down my snow-covered steps. "Say hi to Frank. I hope he's feeling better, soon. See you Monday morning at Lucy's?" I said, referring to the weekly Loopy Lady hooking get together.

"Wouldn't miss it." She waved over her shoulder as tugged the can up her drive.

"Give him a big hello from me, too," Candie said.

Both Candie and I smiled as we returned Gladys's wave and climbed into my Bug. Because of its distinctive yellow color, Candie referred to it as an egg yolk on wheels. But it was mine, paid for, and I loved it.

A few minutes later, the bell over the door of The Ewe jingled, announcing our arrival. "Umph," I cried, bumping into a figure bundled up from head to toe against the outside cold. "I'm sorry." I bent to pick up the package I'd knocked out of her hands.

A muffled "It's okay" emerged from behind a scarf wrapped around her mouth.

I blinked then recognized the winter Michelin Man. "Mari, I'm so sorry. You all right?"

She nodded then hurried out the door.

Candie shook her head. "Strange."

"Her behavior? I agree, but then, she's always acted a little odd." I shrugged and walked into the warmth of the store.

"Hi, ladies. What brings you out on a cold night like this?" Lucy stepped into the main room of The Ewe. "I was folding a batch of wool I dyed this afternoon."

"Um, I need more wool, so I thought I'd check to see if you have any of the mustardy-yellow I'm using for a portion of the background of Porkchop's rug," I said, trying to think of an excuse for us visiting her store.

"You're in luck. I dyed some yellows earlier. Come on back." Lucy led the way into her dye room.

"Lucy, where did you put the butter knife? I need it to make my sandwich. Oh, hi ladies. Want to join me in a gourmet sandwich? If I can find the knife that Lucy hid from me." Ralph turned towards us as we entered the dye room. He grasped a jar of peanut butter in his hand.

CHAPTER TWENTY-EIGHT

"Oh." I clutched the edge of a wooden table stacked with piles of freshly dyed wool fabric.

"Sam, what's the matter? You're whiter than Memaw's boiled rice. Sit down." My cousin pulled out a chair from the table and pushed me into it.

"Thanks." I ran a trembling hand through my hair. The sight of Ralph holding the jar of peanut butter startled me. Visions of Porkchop lying limp on the ground in my backyard flashed before my eyes. Did Ralph drug my Porkie?

"Take a sip of this. Do you need us to take you to the ER?" Lucy hovered at my side with a glass of water.

I waved the glass away. "No, I'm fine."

"Okay. If you say so. I spent most of last night in the ER with Mr. Peanut Butter and Jelly here." Lucy jerked her thumb towards Ralph.

"What?" I asked, straightening up.

"Yep, around five yesterday, right before closing time. Ralph decided he was hungry and decided to make himself a sandwich, but he managed to slice his finger to the bone in the process." Lucy glanced at her blushing husband.

I took a closer look and saw the pointer finger on his left hand heavily bandaged.

"Now Lucy, it's not like I did it on purpose. Sam, I always cut my sandwiches into four triangles. It's how my mom did it when I was a kid and the way I still like mine. A last-minute customer came into the shop, and well, I got distracted and sliced my finger good." Ralph raised the digit in question for my inspection.

Candie shivered. "My lands, it had to have hurt something awful."

"It did, at first, and looked pretty bad. It bled something fierce, so I knew it would take a few stitches," Ralph said.

Lucy shook her head. "Yeah, I grabbed a bunch of paper towels and told him to wrap it up good and not to bleed all over my newly dyed wool."

Candie and I laughed.

"The trouble was, patients packed the ER. I think everyone in Wings Falls suffered some type of emergency last night. My sliced finger sort of put me on the bottom of the priority list in the ER. We sat in the waiting room for over three hours before a PA saw me," Ralph said.

Lucy chuckled. "Do you understand why I've hidden all the knives back here in the kitchen area?"

"I suppose you didn't get out of there until late." I hoped to eliminate Ralph from my suspect list of Porkchop's potential druggers.

Ralph waggled his bandaged finger at us. "By the time they stitched me up and we filled out all the necessary paperwork, we didn't arrive home until after ten."

"Yeah, and since he never did get to eat his PB and J, he wanted to stop at McDonald's before heading home," Lucy said.

Ralph rubbed his stomach. "Hey, my stomach was dancing on my backbone from hunger."

"Porkchop encountered an emergency last night, too." I related to them what had happened the night before.

Lucy's hand flew to her mouth. "How horrible!"

"How's the little fellow doing now?" Ralph asked.

"Fine. He needed a bunch of cuddling today, which I happily showered on him. Are those the wools you dyed this morning, Lucy?" I pointed to a pile of muted yellows sitting on the edge of the table.

"Yes," she said.

I grabbed two off the top of the stack. "I better get back home. I don't want to leave Porkchop alone for too long." Having eliminated Ralph and, by extension, Lucy, of doing any harm to my dog, I didn't have a reason to linger any longer at The Ewe.

"Let me ring up your wool. You found what you need, right?"

I nodded and said, "Yes."

We followed Lucy into her front room, where I paid her for my purchase.

"Here, give this to my little buddy." Ralph held out one of the rawhide bones he kept stashed under the counter for Porkchop's visits.

"He'll love it." Relief swept through me knowing that Ralph truly loved my dog and would never harm him.

I reached for the doorknob then turned to Ralph. "Be a good boy and take care of your finger like the PA instructed. You wouldn't want it to get infected."

Lucy laughed and Ralph blushed. "I'll make sure he follows orders. Give Porkchop a hug from us."

"Will do." I pulled open the shop door. The bell attached overhead jingled. Candie and I waved goodbye.

Darkness had set in, and the night temperature had dropped since we'd entered The Ewe.

"Geez, it's as cold as moonlight on a tombstone," Candie said, stepping onto the sidewalk. "So, what do you think? Innocent or guilty?"

"Innocent." I tugged the collar of my poufy coat up around my ears. "He spent the night in the ER, so that scratches him off the list. Lucy, too, since she sat with him."

Candie pulled her mittens out of her coat pocket and tugged them on. "I agree," she said.

"You know, while I want to find Hilda's killer and sooner rather than later, I'm relieved it isn't those two. Yeah, Ralph has, or should I say professed, no love for Hilda after what she did to his brother, but I could never imagine him harming Porkchop."

Candie slid into my car. "You're right, cuz. He wouldn't shed a tear for Hilda, but he'd do anything for Porkie. We'd better go. Mark plans to come over tonight, and I want to look my best."

* * *

Ten minutes later, I pulled into my drive with my mission accomplished. I felt better knowing my good friends had never harmed my buddy.

I turned in my seat and hugged Candie. My cousin would follow me anywhere, even on my mission to find a murderer. The night was still young, so I asked, "Are you and Mark going out?"

"No, I plan on a night filled with a lot of snuggling by the fire." I swear her eyes twinkled. That old love bug had bit Candie hard, whether she knew it or not.

I laughed. "Sounds like a plan."

Candie stepped out of my car. "Hank coming over?"

I smiled, thinking of my handsome detective. "I hope so. This murder has him tied up, though."

"If he can make it, what are your plans?" Candie reached into the car for her pocketbook.

I walked around to her side of the car. "I kind of like what you have in mind. A whole lot of cuddling by the fire. Thanks for coming with me tonight, cuz."

"Sugar, always. You're not going to play Nancy Drew without me. We're the Sleuth Cousins, remember?"

Candie and I laughed then hugged each other again.

My eyes misted as my gaze followed her down my drive to her baby blue Mustang, Precious. I waved until she drove out of sight then turned and walked back to my house where my barking burglar alarm greeted me. His tail wagged a mile a minute in happiness.

"Hi sweetie. You look fully recovered. Your Uncle Ralph sent you a present." Porkchop barked and jumped at my bag from The Ewe. He sniffed out the bone Ralph sent home and started to happily chew on it.

I shrugged out of my coat and hung it on the hook by the front door. Next, I kicked off my boots and slipped my cold feet into a pair of slippers.

"Come on, Porkie. I need a cup of hot chocolate." He trotted next to me into the kitchen. One would never guess that less than twenty-four hours ago, I feared for his life.

We—me with my cup of hot chocolate and Porkchop clutching the bone between his teeth—retreated into the den. I curled up on the sofa and mulled over my list of suspects. I mentally crossed Ralph and Lucy off the list. That left, as far as I could figure out, Jane and Roberta. Both harbored strong reasons for wanting Hilda dead. Each involved losing a lot of money, a good motive for wanting to get even with someone, possibly kill them.

"Sam, it's me. Where are you?" a voice called out, jerking me awake. I had fallen asleep on the sofa. My hot chocolate sat cold on the table next to me. Porkchop barked and ran into the living room.

"In the den," I shouted, running a hand through my mop of curls. Why did he always have to catch me looking like I had just rolled out of bed?

Hank stood in the doorway of the den, the key to my house that I gave him last fall was clutched in his right hand and a piece of paper in his left. A scowl marred his face. "Sam, what have you been up to?" He held up the crumpled piece of paper.

"What have you got there?" I frowned and pushed myself off the sofa.

"A note I found taped to your front door." In a gloved hand, he held the note out for me to read.

I scanned the note and gasped. *Mind your own business or you'll be next!*

CHAPTER TWENTY-NINE

———

Tears sprang to my eyes.

"Why me?" I searched Hank's handsome face for an answer.

He stepped closer and folded his arms around me. The scent of his spicy aftershave enveloped me. He stroked my back. "I think you know the answer to that question."

I nodded. My cheek glided along the soft polar fleece of his jacket. "I know, poking my nose where it's going to be nipped."

"'Fraid so, sweetheart," he whispered against my hair.

"But Hank, today I only went to The Ewe with Candie," I said, my voice muffled against his chest.

"And the reason for going there…?"

Hank was determined to pry out of me why I went to The Ewe. His Spidey sense spun overtime.

"If I said it was for more wool for the rug I'm hooking, would you believe me?" I raised my head and stared into his crystal-blue eyes.

"Yes and no." He led me over to the sofa.

He sat, pulled me down next to him, and gathered me into his arms. The terror of reading the note started to fade as I cuddled against him.

Porkchop jumped up onto the sofa and snuggled next to us. Laughing, I patted his head.

"Oh, I believe you needed more wool. As you often tell me, a hooker can never have enough wool, but why do I get the idea the visit involved more than adding to your stash?"

"Weeelll, maybe I wanted to check out where Ralph was last night," I said, drawing circles on his chest with the tip of my finger.

Hank sucked in his breath. He placed his large hand over mine to still my finger's movements.

"In a bit," he whispered into my ear. He used his tongue to encircle it. "First, tell me about your trip to The Ewe."

I shivered and scooted back a few inches. If I wanted my brain to think straight, I needed to put a little distance between us.

"Ralph knows Porkie loves rawhide bones. He always gives him one when we visit The Ewe, so it niggled at my brain that maybe, possibly, and I hated to think about it, but could he have committed the murder? You know he has plenty of motive—Hilda stealing Lucy's designs and how she dumped his brother years ago, which led to his brother's suicide. Lucy as much as told us that Ralph blames—blamed—Hilda for his brother's death. So Candie and I decided to *investigate* him a wee bit." I put air quotes around investigate.

"Candie? You dragged your cousin into this, too? Mark isn't going to be too pleased about her getting involved. Especially with him running for reelection." Hank's voice dripped with disapproval.

My back stiffened. "I didn't drag Candie anywhere. And there's one thing both you and Mark need to learn. Candie and I are family, and we Parkers stick together through the good and the bad." I poked him in the chest where moments before I'd drawn lazy circles.

"Okay, okay." Hank threw up his arms. "So, what did you discover from your trip to The Ewe?"

I related everything, from my practically knocking down Mari Adams to Ralph's mishap with a knife.

Hank frowned. "It certainly does narrow the field of suspects if Ralph and Lucy spent the evening in the ER. By the way, who is Mari Adams?"

"Oh, a fellow hooker. She's not one of the Loopy Ladies but is part of Hilda Pratt's group. She's hooking a memory rug of Hilda. She needed some wool. I literally barreled into her as I entered The Ewe," I said, yawning.

"Come on. Enough talk about this case. I hate to admit it, Sam, but you have helped by eliminating Ralph and Lucy from the suspect list." Hank stood and reached down for my hand, gently pulling me off the sofa.

A wide grin spread across my face at his begrudging compliment.

"It doesn't mean I'm in favor of your snooping, but I guess I can't stop you two. Promise me one thing, though," he said, leading the way down the hall to my bedroom.

My body throbbed with excitement at what was to come. I would have promised him anything at this point. "What?"

Midway down the hall, Hank stopped and pulled me into his arms. "You and your sidekick need to be careful. I care too much about you to have anything happen to you. I don't know if I could survive," he said, his voice laced with desperation.

Tears sprang to my eyes as I hugged him to me. "I promise, Hank. With all my heart, I promise."

* * *

My nose twitched. Coffee. I smelled coffee. "*Umpf.*" I raised one sleepy eyelid. "Good morning to you, too, Porkie," I said as he jumped around the tumbled sheets and blankets. He tried to burrow under the covers as only a true doxie would. Hank must have laid him on the bed when he got up.

"Hey, buddy, move over."

Both my eyes opened at the sound of the voice's owner. A smile of complete contentment spread over my face, remembering my night in Hank's capable arms. He placed a mug of coffee on the end table next to the bed. I scooted over so he could sit on the edge. He smelled of the pine scented soap I kept in the shower for him. He'd combed back his wet hair, except for that stubborn brown curl falling across his forehead. I reached up and tucked it into place. He placed his strong hand over mine and moved it to his mouth, where he placed a lingering kiss on the palm of my hand. My eyes closed and a whimper escaped my lips.

Hank stood. "Later, sweetheart. The station called, and I need to get there. It's early. Not even six."

I squinted at my alarm clock. It read 5:45. I hadn't heard his phone ring. "Why so early? Did something happen?" I took a sip of the coffee he'd brewed.

"Yeah, someone committed another home invasion last night. We've experienced a string of them lately," he said, strapping on his service revolver.

I wasn't aware of any home burglaries. What was becoming of my safe hometown—a murder last year and another this year and now home invasions. "Burglaries? As in more than one?"

"Yeah, we think it's a few teens who either needed money for drugs or wanted some kicks." Hank pulled on his fleece jacket.

I shook my head. "Kicks? I guess we acted pretty dull as teens. We toilet-papered a house or left a bag of dog poop on a front porch."

Hank chuckled. "Yeah, the good old days." He leaned down and kissed the top of my head.

I reached up and pulled him close for a proper kiss. One he wouldn't forget for the rest of the day.

Taking a deep breath, he asked, "What's on your agenda today?"

"Thought I'd check out the clearance sale on purses at the Clothes Horse," I said, mentioning my favorite shopping spot on Main Street in Wings Falls.

Hank grinned. He knew my obsession for purses.

What I didn't mention to him, my quest to check out another one of my suspects.

* * *

I pushed open the glass door of the Clothes Horse, smiled, and raised my eyes heavenward. I sent prayers of thanks to the designer purse god for my good fortune. I'd scored. The bag clutched in my hand contained a new red Michael Kors purse. Got it for half price. If I didn't think people would stare at me as if I were a crazy lady, I would have done a happy dance right here on Main Street.

Now to do some snooping or, in my mind, necessary sleuthing. Down the block from the Clothes Horse stood what I thought the most important building in Wings Falls, our library. A stately, two-story brick building, built in the 1880s by the town's benefactor, Charles Wing. The building had expanded over the years with additions, so it now occupied a full city block of Wings Falls. I pushed open one of the large glass doors that led into the main lobby of the library and walked up to the front desk.

A petite blonde-haired woman, in her thirties if I guessed correctly, glanced up at me from a computer screen. "Oh hi, sorry, Sam. I'm trying to catch up on some overdue accounts. Gee, I haven't seen you in ages."

I frowned. The woman looked familiar, but I couldn't place her. "I'm sorry. Do I know you?"

The librarian laughed. "We haven't seen each other in a while. Penny Richards. You used to babysit me. I moved away for a long time but returned back to Wings Falls recently."

I joined in Penny's laughter. "It has been a long time, and you were what, ten the last time I saw you?"

Penny nodded. "Yes. What can I do for you?"

"Is Jane Burrows here today?" I asked, feeling all my fifty-plus years at seeing Penny grown up.

"I believe so. Do you want me to buzz her office to check?" Penny's hand hovered over a phone sitting on the desk next to her computer.

I waved my hand and said, "No, she and I rug hook together. I know the way to her office."

As I weaved my way through the stacks of books to Jane's office, I racked my brain trying to figure a way to ask her about Hilda's death and if she had killed her. I couldn't say, "And by the way, Jane, did you kill Hilda, and with plenty of reason? You know, with her pushing through that dirt bike course, causing you and your mom to have to sell your house at a loss." I laughed out loud. Yeah, like she'd confess to me if she'd done the deed. *Subtle, Sam. You need to be subtle.* Maybe I needed to tune into a few more *CSI* episodes to hone my grilling techniques.

"Want to share the joke, Sam?" said a voice behind me. I jumped as it startled me out of my reverie.

I caught my breath. "Jane, you're the person I wanted to see."

"Sorry to frighten you, but you looked lost in thought." Jane tugged at her navy cardigan sweater.

Think fast, idiot. You have to come up with a reason for being here. "Umm, yes, I got a great deal on a designer purse at the Clothes Horse. You know me and my passion for purses, but now I must earn the money to pay for it. I need to do some research for an article in *Kids Science Magazine.*"

Jane laughed. "You and your purses. Come on into my office, and I'll let you use my computer to research the library's catalog. It'll be more private in there."

"Jane, you're a peach. We can catch up on what you're hooking, too." I followed Jane into her office. Like her simple wardrobe of cardigan sweaters and khaki pants, her office décor was bare bones. Papers were stacked neatly on a corner of her desk. A bookcase stood along one wall holding publishers' catalogs. One of her hooked rugs, a vase holding tulips, hung on the wall opposite the bookcase.

I pointed to the rug. "I always liked the pattern. You did a great job on it, Jane."

"Thanks. Here, take a seat at my desk. I want to check on some books we received this morning. Be back in a few minutes." Jane ran a hand through her short pixie cut and left her office.

Great. Now what? I thought. Jane escaped my questioning. Oh well. I might as well take advantage of her computer offer. I did have an article to research. I lowered myself into the swivel chair and scanned the desktop. Nothing looked unusual there. I pulled open the desk drawer. My eyes widened. *Eureka,* my brain screamed. Look what stared back at me!

CHAPTER THIRTY

———

My fingers shook as I edged the piece of paper out of the drawer. My eyes scanned a receipt from the Ames Chemical Company, an order for an eight-ounce bottle of arsenic. Eight ounces! Geez, how many people had Jane planned to do in? Absentmindedly, I reached for a handful of M&M's from a bowl that sat on her desk. Munching on the candy, I noticed the date she had placed the order. February fifteenth, way before Lucy's hook-in.

"How is your research coming?"

Coughing on the candy, I jerked my head back, and heat crept up my neck. "Um, I needed a pen. Silly me, I forgot mine. To, you know, take notes on the info about traffic signals. What's that old saying? 'Never leave home without a pen'." What a lame explanation. I did a mental palm plant.

Jane walked up to her desk and cocked her head at the blank computer screen staring at me. "Traffic signals?" she asked, leaning a hip against her desk.

"Yeah, for the article I'm writing," I said. Oh no, she'd caught me.

Jane grinned. "Wouldn't it help if you turned on the computer?"

"I know, but I forgot to ask for your password," I stammered. Lying is so not my strong suit. My mom always knew when I tried to fib.

"Bingo," Jane said.

"Bingo?" I repeated like a parrot, not sure what she meant.

"Yep, as in the bingo games Mother and I go to at the fire hall." Jane reached over and pulled the receipt for the arsenic out of my hands.

"Were you and your mother playing bingo two nights ago?" I asked.

"Of course. Fire would have to start in the hall before she would miss her bingo games."

I nodded and thought, *I bet it didn't hurt to have some cute firemen call out the numbers, too.* "How late do the games run?"

"Oh, Mother and I don't get home until after ten. After the last bingo game, we stop for a late-night cup of coffee and doughnut at the 7-Eleven."

Drat! If she and Mommy stopped at the 7-Eleven that late, it eliminates them as possible suspects in harming my Porkie.

"Having a cup of coffee that late would keep me up half the night," I said, pushing away from Jane's desk.

Jane laughed. "Mother and I only have decaf, or we'd stay up to all hours, too."

I nodded towards the receipt she clutched in her hands. "I noticed you ordered some arsenic."

"Oh, yes." She looked at the paper. "Remember that class Lucy gave on dying fabric with arsenic?"

What did it have to do with her ordering a bottle?

"I would like to hold a similar class here at the library. Of course, I would do the demonstrating and have it open only to adults."

"Of course," I agreed. If she used the arsenic to teach a class, I could probably cross her off my suspect list, but I needed to ask one more question. Not knowing the meaning of subtle, I blurted it out. "Jane, during the hook-in, I noticed you left our table for a while."

Turning a bright shade of red, she coughed and pulled at the collar of her cardigan sweater. "I visited Jim Turner in his office."

Jim Turner held the title of the chief of the Wings Falls fire company. A widower with receding gray hair and a sight paunch but one of the nicest men in town. Confusion crossed my face. "Jim Turner's office?" I asked.

Jane stared at the floor. "Yes, we've been dating for a few months now."

I sat speechless. Jane dating—and Jim Turner, no less. My mouth formed into an *O*.

Jane's spine stiffened. She tugged at the bottom of her cardigan. "Don't act so surprised. I'm not so undesirable. I may be 'Plain Jane,' but Jim finds me attractive."

I stood and placed an arm around her shoulder. "Oh, Jane, I'm sure he does, and I didn't mean anything by my reaction. I'm very happy for you and Jim. What does your mother say?"

"Oh, she was surprised at first, but she wants me to be happy and she's become fond of Jim. Especially, since he brings her a box of chocolate-covered cherries whenever he comes over."

I laughed. "I'd love a box, too. I won't take up any more of your time. I'll do my research in the computer area and leave you to your office."

"Are you sure?" Jane asked.

"Very sure. And I'm happy for you and Jim." I hugged Jane then left her office with a smile on my face. I heaved a sigh of relief because I could scratch her off my suspect list and knew that she dated a nice guy, Jim Turner. But I did need to do research for an article on the inventor of the stoplight if I wanted to pay for my purse.

* * *

I stretched then yawned. I glanced at my watch, and my eyes flew open. Was I bent over a computer for two hours? It looked like it, but I hadn't spent all my time researching on the computer. Between trips to the ladies' room and checking out books on Garrett Morgan, the young Black man who invented the first traffic signal in 1923, I'd completed my first draft for my article. A cup of coffee called to me. I gathered up the books I wanted to check out then signed off the computer and hurried to the checkout station.

Umph! "Oh, my goodness. I'm so sorry," I said, fumbling with my armload of books. In my haste, I cut off another library patron making her way to the same checkout station. I caused her to drop her books. The hood of her coat covered her head, so maybe she didn't notice me, but I did feel responsible for the accident. "Here, let me help you." I leaned over to help retrieve the books sprawled on the tiled floor.

"Thank you, Sam, but I think I'm at fault. I'm in a hurry to get home and work on my rug. I needed a little inspiration, so I thought I'd check on the library's rug hooking books."

I glanced up at the owner of the voice and discovered it belonged to Mari Adams. Smiling, I said, "This is the second time I've bumped into you." I took a closer look at the books I helped retrieve off the floor and discovered she indeed had found books on rug hooking.

"Second time?" The hood to Mari's coat slipped off her head revealing matted, greasy hair.

"Yeah, remember, I almost knocked you over at Lucy's place?" As I studied her closer, I noticed her normally pale complexion had taken on a gray hue. Most importantly, she never left home without makeup. Now, her face showed not a trace of it.

"Are you all right?" I asked, handing her a book.

"Yes, fine. I'm fine." A shaking hand took the book from me. "Hilda's death rattled me."

I nodded. "Yes, a big shock. You and Hilda were best friends."

"You have no idea," she said, frowning.

"Here, you go ahead and check out. You're in a hurry, and I have plenty of time." I motioned for her to use the book scanner.

After saying goodbye to Mari and checking out my books, I decided to stroll over to Sweetie Pie's. I needed a cup of coffee. And possibly a slice of her chocolate cream pie to go along with it.

When I pushed open the cafe's door, a tsunami of delicious smells hit me. Hamburgers sizzled on the grill. Maybe I'd quiet my rumbling stomach with one before ordering my pie. After all, I did have a hard morning, purse shopping and researching the article, not to mention doing some sleuthing. I smiled to myself, happy to know that I could cross Jane off my suspect list and more than happy to know she'd found romance. The aroma of freshly brewed coffee curled my toes.

"Hi Sam," Franny greeted me. "Here, I have an empty booth by the window."

I followed her to the booth where I would sit and people watch as I ate.

"I'll send a waitress over to take your order," she said, turning a mug over and pouring the nectar of the gods into it.

"Thanks." After she left, I stared out the window and gazed at people bustling down the street. I loved Wings Falls and couldn't ever imagine living anywhere else.

"Hi, Sam."

I snapped back to the present and turned. Roberta Holden stood next to my table. Her cheeks were red from the cold, and her blonde curls bounced around her shoulders. A smile spread across her face. Could outgoing, friendly Roberta have murdered Hilda? Now was a good time to find out.

"Hi, Roberta. Care to join me for lunch?"

CHAPTER THIRTY-ONE

———

I pointed to the empty red vinyl bench seat across from me.

"Sure." Smiling, she accepted my invitation and slid into the seat. She dumped her packages and purse next to her.

"I guess we've both been shopping." I laughed and pointed to my bag from the Clothes Horse.

"Isn't it the greatest sale they're having? I couldn't resist some of their bargains. I'll need to sneak some of these bags past Clyde. I don't want his blood pressure to spike even higher." Roberta shrugged out of her down coat and placed it on top of her purchases.

"Clyde has a blood pressure problem?" I asked, frowning. "I didn't know."

Roberta nodded. "Ever since Hilda gave us that bad investment advice, his blood pressure has climbed."

"Geez, I'm sorry about his blood pressure. Did his doctor put him on meds?" I remembered how they'd trusted Hilda and lost money when she pointed them to some "get rich quick" investments. Would the bad advice make Roberta angry enough to have killed Hilda? Maybe Clyde's high blood pressure pushed her over the edge?

"Hi, ladies. Ready to order?"

A new girl, one I didn't recognize, stood poised next to our table with a pen and order pad in her hand. The name tag pinned to the handkerchief flowing out of her breast pocket read Robin. The 50s-style waitress uniform fit her slim body to a T.

"Hi, Robin. I think I'll have the hamburger special. Loaded with catsup, onions, and tomatoes. I would like a side of fries, too, please." I handed her my menu then nodded at Roberta.

"I'll have the same. Did Franny make some of her delish cider doughnuts this morning?" Roberta glanced up at Robin with hopeful eyes.

Robin laughed. "She did. I'll check, but I can't promise anything. I don't know if the morning crowd left any."

Roberta turned her attention to me. "I'm addicted to those doughnuts."

'"You aren't the only one. I think she's hooked most of Wings Falls. They ought to be outlawed. I might ask Hank what he can do about declaring those doughnuts illegal," I said, laughing.

With a look of mock horror on her face, Robin held up her hands. "No, please no. I beg of you. Our morning customers would riot." She tucked her pen behind her ear, placed the order book in her apron pocket, and turned towards the kitchen.

"I read your latest column in the *Senior Chatter.* Sounds like the last town council meeting got a little heated." Roberta, besides teaching classes at The Ewe, covered the town council meetings for the senior center's newspaper, the *Senior Chatter.* She did a good job keeping Wings Falls' older population informed about what the town elders did or didn't do with their tax dollars.

She pushed her cherry-red glasses up her nose and leaned across the table closer to me. "I swear if it weren't for Hank attending the meeting, calming things down, a knockdown, drag-out brawl would have erupted."

I smiled and recalled Hank telling me about the meeting. Apparently, the owner of the dirt bike park wanted to reopen the track this summer. He said he had a new backer, and it would be a success this time. He also wanted to increase his hours of operation. "Hank told me about it. Can't say that I blame the neighbors of the dirt bike park for being upset. The park caused nothing but trouble when it was open before. I can't imagine the town council giving it a second okay to reopen."

"You're right. I mean, look what it did to poor Jane and her mother. They had to practically give their home away when they wanted to sell. No one wanted to live next to all the noise that the dirt bikes created," Roberta said, taking a sip of her coffee.

"So, Roberta, have Clyde's blood pressure meds worked?" I wanted to steer the conversation back to her and if she harbored a reason to murder Hilda.

Red crept up into Roberta's face. "As I said, his blood pressure has soared since Hilda cheated us out of a big part of our savings."

"Do you think she did it on purpose?" I asked.

Roberta sank back in her seat, deflated. "I don't know. Maybe, maybe not, but if she didn't know what she was doing, she shouldn't have urged us to invest. Ugh. Every time I think of her, I need a cigarette to calm my nerves."

My eyes widened. "So, you went out back of the firehouse to have a smoke at the hook-in?"

Roberta blushed. "Yeah, I'm afraid so. Stress has me backsliding sometimes, but I'm trying hard to kick the habit. I haven't smoked since then."

I smiled. "Good for you, but can I ask you a question about your whereabouts two nights ago?"

Her face lit up. "Oh, an easy one. Clyde and I celebrated our anniversary with dinner at Momma Mia's then spent the rest of the evening snuggling on the sofa enjoying a delicious bottle of Chablis and listening to romantic music. Why do you want to know?"

"Um, no reason. You know me. I'm a curious creature."

Roberta stared at me as if I'd lost a marble or two, but it was okay because my mind did a silent happy dance. If she and Clyde had spent the evening snuggling on the sofa listening to romantic music and doing whatever, I could cross her off my list of suspects who wanted to harm Porkchop and kill Hilda.

Robin returned with our lunch. "Here you go, ladies. Two orders of burgers and fries."

All thoughts of murder flew out of my mind as I looked at the plates piled high with juicy burgers and fries.

"I'll return later with those cider doughnuts and more coffee," Robin said, leaving us to our meal.

* * *

"So, tell me again why you're dragging me to The Ewe? I know we don't need an excuse to buy more wool, but I'm expecting Mark soon, and I have to make sure I'm presentable," my dear cousin complained from the passenger seat of my Bug.

I had called her earlier and told her about my lunch with Roberta, but I wanted to go over our conversation again in case I was dismissing Roberta as a murder suspect too prematurely. Candie needed to make a quick stop at the CVS, and me—some more wool. With only a few more inches to hook on my rug, I had run out of the red for my background. Hank worked tonight, and I thought I'd spend my alone time finishing my rug. "I told you I wanted to recap my conversation with Roberta today at Sweetie Pie's. Do you think we can X her off the suspect list?"

Candie flipped down her visor and slid open the mirror. She pulled out a tube of Passion Pink lipstick and ran it across her lips. After inspecting her lips in the mirror, she said, "Yes, honey, I think we can. I wish we could solve this mystery and not have to regard every hooker as if she had killed Hilda."

I nodded in agreement. I hated thinking one of my friends could possibly have murdered Hilda.

I nabbed a parking space in front of The Ewe. We got out of my Bug and entered our home away from home.

"It's only us," I called out as we walked into the main room. The jingling bell over the door also announced our entrance.

Lucy emerged from the dye room, a bundle of red wool in her arms. "Hi, ladies. Glad you could make it before we closed."

"Thanks, Lucy, for staying open until we got here." I pointed to the wool in her arms. "Any chance my wool is in there?"

Lucy handed the wool over to me.

"Yeah, she has cut into my primping time," Candie muttered next to me.

"Hot date tonight, Candie?" Lucy asked.

"Darling, every date with Mark is a hot one." Candie batted her eyelashes at Lucy.

"Let me pay for my wool so you can close up." I reached into my pink Kate Spade cross-over purse for my wallet.

Lucy laughed. "Oh, no hurry. Ralph and I have a hot date tonight, too, sitting in front of the TV with some pizza. By the way, would it be a bother if you drop some wool off at Mari's place on your way home?"

"No problem at all. Unfortunately, I don't have any plans tonight. Hank has to work, so it's Porkchop, me, and my hooking frame." I handed Lucy the exact amount I owed her for my wool.

* * *

"Aren't you little Miss Congeniality. I told you I needed to get home to make myself luscious for Mark. Now we've got to swing by Mari's house. Hon, this better be a drop and run." Candie drummed her fingers on the Bug's armrest that separated the two of us. She was clearly agitated with me.

A few minutes later, we arrived at Mari's. "Oh, Candie, come on. We pass Mari's house on the way to the CVS, and besides, you are already beautiful. You'll knock Mark's socks off." No exaggeration there. My cousin's auburn hair curling around her porcelain skin made her a true beauty.

Candie pouted. "Promise you'll only be a sec?" Her phone rang. She pulled her bejeweled phone out of her purse and scanned her caller ID. A smile spread across her face. "Speak of the devil. It's my sweet peach right now." She turned her attention to her phone. "Hi my sugar."

I smiled. Mark didn't stand a chance. I opened my car door and grabbed Mari's wool. I mouthed I'd be right back. My dear cousin sat in the Bug lost in a conversation with her "sugar" and never noticed me leaving.

I stood on the sidewalk leading up to Mari's front door for a second. Her house was once an adorable Craftsman style, but now the paint hung in strips that peeled away from the wood siding. A window on the second floor was cracked. The porch steps creaked as I climbed them. I needed to maneuver around a board missing from the top step.

I knocked on the weathered front door and hoped Mari was home. I didn't want to make a return trip. I guess I could always leave her wool on the wobbly rocker standing at the far end of the porch.

"Hi, Sam, what a surprise." Mari stood framed in the doorway. She clutched a spatula in her right hand and wore a flowered apron.

"Oh, hi, Mari. I've got the wool you ordered from Lucy. She asked me to drop it off."

"How kind of you." A *buzz* sounded. "Oh dear, the timer on my stove is going off. I'm baking brownies for my boys. They love Mom's brownies, even though they don't live here anymore. They always anticipate a care package from home. Be right back." Laughing, Mari turned and dashed to her kitchen.

I stepped inside and glanced around her living room. The condition of it was not much better than the outside of her home—shabby and in dire need of some sprucing up. A worn faded sofa with stuffing poking out of one cushion held court in the center of the room. I noticed her hooking frame set up in a small den off the kitchen. I was curious about the progress of her tribute rug to Hilda. Should I or shouldn't I satisfy my curiosity? Curiosity won out. I wandered into the room for a peek. I stood next to the frame and gasped. My hand shook as I ran it over the loops of wool.

CHAPTER THIRTY-TWO

————

"Would you care to sample one of my brownies? What the…? What are you doing in here?"

I turned. Mari stood in the doorway of the room holding a knife in one hand, a brownie balanced on the long sharp blade.

"You killed Hilda, didn't you?" I glanced over my shoulder at the rug. It depicted Hilda with a rug hook stuck in her neck and blood dripped from it. Except for the police, Candie, and me, no one knew the exact manner of Hilda's death.

Mari's mouth turned into a sneer. "She deserved to die years ago. First, she mesmerized my husband, Mac, so that he'd leave me. Then after he died, she made me grovel for every penny from his estate for my boys. Mac's will left money for their education, but she threatened to change it. She tried to cut them off without a penny. I wouldn't let her ruin my sons' futures."

She acted completely unhinged. Tears streamed down her pale face.

I shook my head in disbelief. "But if his will stated the boys inherited money for their education, how could she change it?"

"She said she found a lawyer who could make the changes. I couldn't let her do that to my boys. I'm sorry, Sam, but I can't let you go now. Not since you've discovered my secret. You wouldn't heed my warnings and stop snooping." Mari advanced towards me with the knife. A panicked giggle escaped me as the brownie fell to the floor. I needed to get a grip and not let hysteria take over.

"It was you who left that note on my door and sliced my tires in Albany." Then realization dawned on me, and anger boiled in my veins. "You laced my Porkchop's bone with that drug, didn't you?"

Tears started to stream down Mari's face. "Honestly, Sam, I didn't want to. But you wouldn't mind your own business and stop asking questions. I had no other choice."

"Mind my own business!" I shouted. "You could have killed my dog."

"Sam, what's taking you so long? You know I have to get home and gorgalicious myself for my date with Mark." Candie came to an abrupt halt in the den's doorway, her cell phone clutched in her hand. "What the…?"

My cousin's appearance distracted Mari. I looked over Mari's shoulder and saw Candie do her famous high school softball wind-up pitch. She flung her bejeweled cell phone and knocked the knife out of Mari's hand. I blinked for one second then sprang into motion and tackled Mari to the floor.

I sat on Mari, reached for Candie's phone lying next to us, and dialed Hank's number. He answered on the first ring. After I relayed what went down at Mari's, he said he was out the door and on the way.

Mari lay beneath me sobbing like a baby, crying over and over, "My boys, my boys." I didn't think she was a threat, so I glanced up at Candie and nodded to a pile of wool sitting next to her hooking frame. "Rip some of Mari's wool into strips so we can tie her up until Hank gets here."

I secured Mari's hands and feet with the wool. I think I pulled the strips a little tighter than needed, but I still seethed thinking of what she had put my Porkchop and me through. I handed Candie her phone.

She took it from me and frowned. "My poor phone. Some of the rhinestones fell off."

I laughed. "Yeah, but you're still the best softball pitcher ever to play at Hainted Holler High."

Candie puffed up. A smile spread across her face. "You bet your ever-lovin' purse passion I am."

* * *

Hank sat next to me at a candlelit table at Momma Mia's. He held my hand as if afraid to let go. Today's events had shaken him about as badly as they had me. My phone pinged, and I scanned the text. "Candie says to expect Mark and her any minute. I know what Mari did was wrong, but I could almost feel sorry for her. Hilda held her in such an evil grip."

Hank took a sip of wine then nodded. "I know, but it still didn't give her the right to take Hilda's life."

"I agree, but in her mind, she was protecting her sons, and a momma will do anything to protect her children." If it was my child, would I do the same in Mari's place?

Hank placed his wineglass on the table and leaned closer to me so our conversation couldn't be heard by other tables. "You were right about Hilda being allergic to arsenic."

I nodded. "Mari knew about Hilda growing up on a farm where arsenic was used to keep away rats. Hilda was aware from childhood about her reaction to even the smallest amounts of arsenic. When Lucy offered the dye class at The Ewe in dying with arsenic, Hilda made a big deal out of why she couldn't take the class. I guess Mari used Hilda's boast to plot her revenge."

* * *

"Hi, y'all. Why so glum?"

I glanced up to Candie smiling from ear to ear, clutching Mark's arm.

"We were discussing Mari and how sad all this turned out," I said. I twirled my glass of wine between my fingers.

Mark pulled a seat out for Candie then seated himself. "Now, we'll have none of those sad thoughts. Tonight, we need to celebrate."

Candie motioned for a passing waiter and asked him to bring us a bottle of champagne.

"Celebrate? What is there to celebrate?" I asked, frowning.

Candie smiled and held up her left hand. A headlight-sized diamond sparkled from her ring finger.

I squealed and jumped up from my chair, ran over, and hugged her. "What? When?" I stuttered.

Candie stared up at Mark. Love sparkled in her eyes. "The little devil, he said he'd bought the ring ages ago, but he wanted to wait for the right moment to pop the question. Well, after today's happenings, Mark said he never wanted to lose me, so he up and proposed. And of course, I said yes."

I clapped my hands. "I'm so happy for you. When do you think you'll have the wedding?"

Candie's eyes locked on to her ring, and then she sent a loving look to her fiancé. "This summer, after Mark's primary for mayor. I'm hoping for July seventh. You know 7/7. Seven is my lucky number."

I laughed. My cousin had a superstitious streak.

Hank reached across the table to shake Mark's hand. "Congratulations, Mark, and to you, too, Candie."

A look of horror spread across Candie's face.

Hank glanced around the table. "What, what? Did I say something wrong?"

I shook my head and laughed, trying to lighten the mood. "It's only an old wives' tale Memaw Parker used to tell us when we were young. You never say congratulations to the bride. It means bad luck."

ABOUT THE AUTHOR

Syrl Ann Kazlo, a retired teacher, lives in upstate New York with her husband and two very lively dachshunds. Kibbles and Death is the first book in her Samantha Davies Mystery series, featuring Samantha Davies and her lovable dachshund, Porkchop. When not writing Syrl is busy hooking—rug hooking that is—reading, and enjoying her family. She is a member of Sisters in Crime and the Mavens of Mayhem.

Learn more about S.A. Kazlo at:
www.sakazlo.com

Made in United States
Cleveland, OH
24 November 2024

10861006R00120